The Rainbow Pool

Born in Hertfordshire, England, on 29 May 1952, Louise Cooper describes herself as 'a typical scatterbrained Gemini'. She spent most of her school years writing stories when she should have been concentrating on lessons, and her first fantasy novel, *The Book of Paradox*, was published in 1973, when she was just twenty years old. Since then she has published more than eighty books for adults and children.

Louise now lives in Cornwall with her husband, Cas Sandall. When she isn't writing, she enjoys singing (and playing various instruments), cooking, gardening, 'messing about on the beach' and – just to make sure she keeps busy – is also treasurer of her local Royal National Lifeboat Institution branch.

Visit Louise at her own website at louisecooper.com

Books by Louise Cooper

Sea Horses series in reading order

Sea Horses
The Talisman
Gathering Storm
The Last Secret

Mermaid Curse series in reading order

The Silver Dolphin
The Black Pearl
The Rainbow Pool

Mermaid Curse

The Rainbow Pool

Louise Cooper

PUFFIN

PUFFIN BOOKS

Published by the Penguin Group
Penguin Books Ltd, 80 Strand, London WC2R ORL, England
Penguin Group (USA) Inc., 375 Hudson Street, New York, New York 10014, USA
Penguin Group (Canada), 90 Eglinton Avenue East, Suite 700, Toronto, Ontario, Canada M4P 2Y3
(a division of Pearson Penguin Canada Inc.)
Penguin Ireland, 25 St Stephen's Green, Dublin 2, Ireland (a division of Penguin Books Ltd)
Penguin Group (Australia), 250 Camberwell Road, Camberwell, Victoria 3124, Australia
(a division of Pearson Australia Group Pty Ltd)
Penguin Books India Pvt Ltd, 11 Community Centre, Panchsheel Park, New Delhi – 110 017, India
Penguin Group (NZ), 67 Apollo Drive, Rosedale, North Shore 0632, New Zealand
(a division of Pearson New Zealand Ltd)
Penguin Books (South Africa) (Pty) Ltd, 24 Sturdee Avenue, Rosebank,
Johannesburg 2196, South Africa

Penguin Books Ltd, Registered Offices: 80 Strand, London WC2R ORL, England

puffinbooks.com

First published 2008
1

Text copyright © Louise Cooper, 2008
All rights reserved

The moral right of the author has been asserted

Set in Sabon
Typeset by Palimpsest Book Production Limited, Grangemouth, Stirlingshire
Made and printed in England by Clays Ltd, St Ives plc

British Library Cataloguing in Publication Data
A CIP catalogue record for this book is available from the British Library

ISBN: 978-0-141-32227-8

www.greenpenguin.co.uk

Penguin Books is committed to a sustainable future
for our business, our readers and our planet.
The book in your hands is made from paper
certified by the Forest Stewardship Council.

To my husband, Cas,
for helping me to get my sea details right . . .
and for a lot of other lovely reasons.

Prologue

The mermaid gazed at Kes with a smile on her face. Black hair with a blue sheen cascaded over her shoulders, and her eyes were brilliant emerald green. Her face was very beautiful, but it was also cruel and spiteful. On her head was a golden circlet set with seven pearls.

'Well?' she demanded. 'Haven't you got anything to say for yourself?' She leaned forward and the look in her eyes made Kes shiver. '*Do you even know who I am?*'

Trembling, Kes managed to find his voice. 'You are . . . Queen Taran . . .' Then a little of his courage crept back and he added, 'Where's

1

my mother? What have you done with her?'

'She's safe and well for now,' Taran replied carelessly. Then her expression changed. 'But, if you want her to *stay* well, you must do as I tell you. Do you understand?'

Kes swallowed and nodded.

'Good. Now, do you know why you've been brought here?'

He shook his head. 'No . . . Your Majesty.'

'It's very simple.' Suddenly Taran reached out and gripped his arm. Kes winced; she was amazingly strong. She stared into his face, and her voice turned from sweetness to venom as she hissed, '*I want the silver pearl!*'

Kes started to shake with fear. 'Th-the . . . silver pearl . . . ?' he echoed.

'Yes! Your sister has it in the locket she wears. And you've seen it, haven't you?'

'No, Your Majesty –'

'Don't lie to me! I *know*!' Taran's voice rose shrilly, then with an effort she got herself under control again. 'I *will* have the silver pearl, Kesson.

And you will help me to get it. Your mother is going to stay here for a while, as my . . . guest.' The way she said the word *guest* made Kes shudder inwardly. 'And you are going to carry out a little errand for me. If you complete it, I will set Morvyr free. But if you fail . . .' She uttered an unpleasant laugh. 'Well, let's just say that you will both regret that very much.'

Finding his voice with an effort, Kes said, 'What do you want me to do?'

'You will go to shore and find your sister,' Taran told him. 'Tell her that your mother is a prisoner, and the silver pearl is the price of her freedom. She must bring it to me!'

With a last shred of defiance Kes said, 'What if she won't?'

'Then you must persuade her. Otherwise, you will never see your mother again. And you don't want that. *Do you?*'

Chapter One

'Come on, Rose, or we'll miss them!' Lizzy
Baxter was almost bouncing with
impatience on the front doorstep. Her short
blonde hair bounced too, its unruly curls gleaming
in the early sunlight.

'All right, I'm coming!' The reply ended in
sounds of a large yawn, then Lizzy's fifteen-year-
old sister appeared. 'And keep your voice down.
Mum and Dad are still asleep.' She blinked in the
brightness and lifted her hands to rub her eyes,
then remembered her newly applied make-up and
stopped herself in time. 'Whose dumb idea was it
to get up at the crack of dawn?'

'You wanted to see the boat off as much as I did,' Lizzy reminded her.

'Yeah, but I'd probably have changed my mind if it wasn't for you pestering me.' Rose yawned again, then her morning grumpiness started to fade and she grinned. 'OK, then, let's go. At least it isn't raining.'

The two girls set off along the street and down the hill that led to the harbour of the Cornish fishing port. 'It's hardly rained at all since we moved here,' Lizzy said as they walked. 'The weather's been lovely all summer, apart from that storm.'

'Yeah, that was unreal.' Then Rose looked sidelong at her. 'Why are you so keen to come to the harbour, anyway? You hardly know Mr Treleaven, so what's the sudden fascination with seeing him and Paul go off on their fishing trip?'

Lizzy watched the local newsagent putting out his paper stands and pretended she hadn't heard. She *did* have a reason for wanting to be at the harbour, and a very good one, but she couldn't tell Rose about it. It had nothing to do with Mr Treleaven, or his son Paul, who was Rose's boyfriend. But someone else was going out on the boat today. And that person was very important to Lizzy.

The Baxters had moved to Cornwall less than a month ago, and Lizzy found it hard to believe that so much had happened to her since then. She and Rose were both adopted – Mr and Mrs Baxter couldn't have children of their own – but though Rose knew all about her real parents, Lizzy's past was a mystery. She had been found abandoned as a baby, and had grown up with no idea who her mother and father were.

Until, just a few days after arriving here, she had met a boy called Kes, and made an astounding discovery. She had lost the mother-of-pearl locket that had been with her when she was abandoned and was the only link she had with her mysterious past. Heartbroken, she had been searching the beach in the slender hope of finding it when Kes had approached her with the locket in his hand. He had guessed that it was Lizzy's, because the lock of hair inside it was the same pale blonde shade as hers. And the hair colour told him something else. It told him that she was his long-lost twin sister.

That alone would have been enough to turn Lizzy's life upside down. But there was far more. For Kes wasn't an ordinary boy. His mother's name was Morvyr, which meant 'daughter of the sea' – and Morvyr was a mermaid.

At first Lizzy had flatly refused to believe it. Mermaids didn't exist – even with her vivid imagination she had grown out of that sort of fairy tale years ago! But Kes had proved the truth to her in a spectacular way: by taking her under the sea, where she discovered that she could breathe as easily as she did on land. It was crazy, it was impossible, but it was true. She was a mermaid's daughter. And when she met Morvyr, and saw her face, and the hair that was exactly the same pale gold as her own, the last of her doubts had vanished.

Rose was hurrying now as she realized that they might be late, and Lizzy had to break into a trot to keep up with her. Her mind went back to the third person who was going out on Mr Treleaven's boat this morning, and her heart gave a little inward skip at the thought of seeing him again. His name was Jack Carrick – and he was her real father.

Jack Carrick had been born and brought up in this town. He was a fisherman, and he, like Lizzy, had not believed in mermaids. But then, years ago, he had had an accident while out sailing. He would have drowned, but Morvyr had seen what had happened and saved his life. They fell in love and were married in a mermaid ceremony. Jack was human and could not live underwater like Morvyr. But the old Queen of the mermaids – Queen Kara – had been kindly, and had used her magical powers to make a spell that enabled him to stay beneath the sea for short periods of time.

Jack and Morvyr had been blissfully happy . . . until, soon after the twins were born, Lizzy had been stolen. Believing that she had been taken far across the sea, Jack went in search of her, and for eleven years nothing more was heard of him. Morvyr had feared he was dead. But, a week ago, Jack had returned – and Lizzy had met her true father for the first time.

Rose's voice brought her suddenly back to earth. 'What's up with you? You look as if you've just swallowed a wasp.'

Lizzy realized that the thoughts running through her mind were showing in her expression, and quickly she made her face relax. 'Sorry,' she said. 'I was trying to get something out from between my teeth.'

'Yuk! Spare me the gory details.' They had reached the foot of the hill, and could now see the dock with its wharves and packing sheds and covered fish market. 'Look, there's Mr Carrick,' Rose added, pointing. 'See – on the harbour wall. Come on, or we'll be too late!'

Lizzy's heart skipped again, but she was careful not to let her eagerness show. She and Jack had agreed that no one else must know their secret. It was hard for Lizzy – she wanted to celebrate, to be able to call Jack 'Dad'. But the thought of trying to explain to her adoptive parents, the Baxters, was too awful to contemplate. How would they feel if they knew the truth? They were the only mother and father Lizzy had ever known, and she loved them dearly. She couldn't hurt them by suddenly announcing that she had found her real father and he was living here in this very town. As for Morvyr . . . to tell anyone about her was absolutely impossible. So Lizzy must pretend that Jack was just someone she happened to know. Luckily he was staying with the Treleavens, who were his old friends, so if he and Lizzy were seen talking together, no one would think it strange. But deep down Lizzy knew that things couldn't go on like this forever.

The girls ran to the harbour and hurried on to

the quay. Jack Carrick had seen them and waited for them to catch up.

'Morning, Rose. You're an early bird. Hello, Lizzy.' His eyes were warm as he looked at her. 'Come to see us off? That's nice.'

The three of them walked on together, to where Mr Treleaven and Paul were making final preparations to put to sea. Their boat was called *Regard*; she was small enough to operate with two crewmen, but Jack had jumped at the chance for a fishing trip. 'Reminds me of my young days,' he had said to Lizzy yesterday.

Paul came scrambling over fishing gear and coiled ropes, and jumped ashore to greet Rose. 'You made it, then?' he teased. 'I thought you'd still be in bed.'

'I probably would, only Lizzy dragged me out. She had a bee in her bonnet about wanting to come too.' Rose went on chattering, and Lizzy sidled closer to Jack. She needed to talk to him privately, and this might be her only chance before the *Regard* put to sea. Lowering her voice, she whispered, 'Have you seen Arhans again?'

Jack's expression clouded. 'Not yet. But if there were any news, she would have come by now.'

Lizzy nodded. 'That's the worst thing, isn't it? Just waiting. I feel so *useless*.'

'Me too. That's why I'm looking forward to this trip; it'll take my mind off other things.' He smiled at her. 'You should try to do the same.'

'I know. I *will* try.' Making sure that none of the others was looking, she briefly clasped his hand and squeezed it. 'But I'll be glad when you get back.'

Mr Treleaven, grinning broadly, was shouting to Paul to stop mooning around and get on board. There were quick farewells all round, then the boat's engine spluttered into life, the mooring ropes were cast off, and *Regard* nosed slowly from her berth and, propellers thrashing the water, turned towards the open sea.

Rose stood waving at Paul's dwindling figure on deck, and Lizzy waved too, though Jack was careful only to wave back once in reply. *Regard* glided between the jutting bulks of the harbour walls, and moved out into Mount's Bay. Another larger trawler was following in her wake, and two more were about to leave.

Rose sighed and turned away at last. 'Oh, well,' she said. 'At least while Paul's gone I can go in to Penzance and do some shopping, if I've got any money left, which I probably haven't.' She stopped, looking back at her sister. 'Lizzy? Are you coming?'

Lizzy did not answer. She was staring at a spot in the harbour, beyond the docks. Something was moving just under the water.

'What is it?' Rose asked. 'What have you – Oh, wow!'

A dolphin had surfaced. It came streaking towards the quay, its dorsal fin making a small bow-wave. Rose watched in astonished delight, then suddenly realized that Lizzy was running along the quay wall towards the creature.

'Lizzy, don't, you'll scare it off!' she shouted.

Lizzy took no notice. She reached the end of the quay, crouched down – and to Rose's surprise, the dolphin swam straight to her. It rose up until it was half out of the water, and Rose could hear the extraordinary noises, like a cross between chattering and creaking, that it made.

'Wow!' she said again. The dolphin must be tame – she couldn't miss out on this! She also started to run, then slowed down in case two people rushing at it were too much for the dolphin. Lizzy was leaning out over the wall, and Rose thought she heard her call out something that sounded like 'Arhans'. *Arhans?* Whatever did that mean?

She didn't know that Arhans was the dolphin's name – and Arhans and Lizzy knew each other very well. Lizzy had recognized the distinctive silver streak that ran the length of Arhans's back, and in her eagerness to see her friend she had forgotten all about Rose.

'Is there any news?' she asked breathlessly. 'Are Kes and Morvyr all right?'

Arhans made more chattering-creaking sounds – chittering, some people called it – and Lizzy felt frustration well up in her. The dolphins understood human speech but she had hardly begun to learn theirs. The sea people could communicate with them, and so could Jack. But whatever Arhans was telling her she didn't understand!

Suddenly she became aware of footsteps behind her, and looked round quickly to see Rose only a few paces away.

'Arhans!' she hissed to the dolphin. 'I can't talk here! The lighthouse – meet me by the lighthouse!'

'Isn't it *gorgeous*!' Rose said breathlessly, gazing at Arhans. 'But, Lizzy, what were you saying to it? What was – Oh!' Arhans had dropped back into the water, turned and with a slap of her tail flukes slid under the surface and vanished, leaving only ripples in her wake.

'It's gone!' Rose's voice was stark with disappointment. 'And I didn't get a proper look at it!'

'You must have frightened her off,' Lizzy replied. There was something strange in her tone, and Rose asked sharply, 'Why "her"? How do you know it was a female? And what *were* you saying to it? That word – Arhans, or something. What does it mean?'

'I don't know what you're on about,' Lizzy said, not looking at her. 'Anyway, the dolphin's gone now.'

'Well, if we wait for a while, it might come back.'

Lizzy shrugged. 'You can if you want. I'm going.'

'Lizzy, wait! *Lizzy!*'

But Lizzy was hurrying away. For a moment or two Rose thought of running after her, but changed her mind. It was just another one of Lizzy's weird moods, she thought. She'd been having them a lot lately, but Rose couldn't work out what was wrong with her and Lizzy wouldn't say. *OK*, she thought, *if she wants to be like that, let her.*

Turning her back on her sister, Rose shoved her hands in her jeans pockets and stared out across the harbour, looking hopefully for the dolphin.

Chapter Two

The small automatic lighthouse where Lizzy had asked Arhans to meet her was set on the low headland that jutted out between the harbour and the beach at the other end of the town. Lizzy ran all the way. She hoped fervently that Arhans would be there. Though she hadn't understood what the dolphin had been trying to tell her, there was obviously some news to tell. Was it about Kes and Morvyr? Lizzy really hoped it was, for she had not seen her mother and brother for days. They were in trouble – and the cause of the trouble was Taran, the mermaid Queen. Taran believed that Morvyr had something she wanted, and in an attempt to get it she had given an order for Morvyr and Kes to be arrested. Luckily the dolphins had warned them in time, and they had gone into hiding. But Lizzy had not heard from them since then . . .

She was relieved, when she reached the top of the cliff path, to see that there was no one else around. It wasn't seven o'clock yet; too early for the August holidaymakers or even local dog-walkers to be out. The wind blew her hair back from her face as she came to a halt beside the lighthouse's white-painted bulk. Out in the bay she could see the departing fishing boats, though they were too far away now for her to tell which one was the *Regard*. Gulls screamed in the distance, and the sun was dazzling. There were a few pinky-coloured clouds low down on the horizon, but apart from that the sky was clear.

When she had got her breath back, she moved round to the seaward side of the lighthouse and looked down. The cliff sloped steeply, and at its foot the sea slapped and foamed over the rocks.

At first she thought there was nothing else there. But then a darker shape showed under the water. Expecting to see Arhans, Lizzy was astonished when, instead, a boy with jet-black hair and eyes as vividly blue as her own appeared.

'*Kes!*' she cried joyfully.

Kes swam to the foot of the cliff and started to climb up towards her. He had willed himself to change from a merboy to fully human shape, and he climbed with an effortless ease that Lizzy envied.

She reached out to help him up the last steep metre and he scrambled on to the grass beside her. 'Oh, Kes, I'm so glad to see you! I've been worried out of my mind! Are you all right?'

She was smiling happily and eagerly, but the smile faded as she saw Kes's grim expression. 'What is it?' she asked in sudden alarm. 'Is Taran still looking for you?'

'It's worse than that.' Kes sat down. He was breathing heavily, as though he had been swimming very fast. 'She captured us.'

'*Captured?*'

He nodded. 'Arhans came to the cave where we were hiding. She told us about Father coming back. It was all my fault, Lizzy – I persuaded Mother not to wait till it was safer, but to go and find him. We left at night; we thought we could get here without being seen. But Tullor caught us.'

'Oh, no . . .' Lizzy had encountered Tullor, the monstrous conger eel who was Taran's most faithful henchman, and the memory made her shiver.

'We couldn't do anything,' Kes went on. 'He had two giant cuttlefish with him; they caught us in their tentacles and – and took us to Taran.' He shut his eyes briefly. 'I think it was some time yesterday. I was unconscious – or she put some kind of spell on me to make me sleep – so I don't know for sure.'

'But you escaped?'

'No. Taran let me go. There's something she wants. If we give it to her, she says she'll set Mother free too. But if we don't . . .' He didn't finish the sentence, but the look in his eyes said everything.

Lizzy whispered starkly, 'She wants the silver pearl.'

'Yes! How did you know?'

'Father told me all about the pearls. There are nine of them, and they were set into Queen Kara's crown. But when Taran stole the crown —'

'So, she's not the real Queen. She *is* a usurper! I knew it; I've always thought it, but no one would ever say — not even Mother.'

'It gets worse,' said Lizzy. 'She's a murderer! She killed Queen Kara. But in the struggle the Queen managed to save two of the pearls, and before she died she gave them to Mother to take care of.'

Kes's face contorted with fury. 'Taran said Mother stole them!'

'Of course she didn't! She hid them, and when Taran couldn't find them, she kidnapped me to try to make Mother tell where they were. Then she laid a false trail so that Father would go far away searching for me.'

'And all the time the silver pearl was hidden in your locket . . .'

'Yes. But, Kes, there's another pearl –'

'I know – a black one. Taran wants that too. If she gets the black and silver pearls, then her crown will be whole again – and she'll have total power!' He paused. 'Father's got the black pearl, hasn't he? Arhans gave us his message, about the ninth one being safe. Is that what he meant?'

She nodded. 'I've seen it. He keeps it in another locket, the one he made for you. He took it with him when he went away.' She unzipped the top of her fleece and pulled out her own locket, which hung on a silver chain round her neck. The locket was beautifully made from mother-of-pearl shells; Lizzy pressed the catch and it sprang open. Kes looked alarmed, and she said, 'Don't worry. The silver pearl's in the secret compartment – it's perfectly safe. This is what I wanted to show you.'

Inside the locket, together with a curl of their mother's golden hair, was a small piece of paper, tightly folded until it was hardly bigger than a pea.

Lizzy smoothed it out and showed it to Kes. 'It's a rhyme. Father wrote it down for me.'

He peered, then shook his head. 'I don't understand.'

'It's writing,' said Lizzy. Then suddenly she realized why he was so puzzled. Of course – Kes had grown up under the sea, so he had never been to school. He couldn't understand the idea of writing.

She smiled at him a little sadly as she thought how different their lives had been, and said, 'Father said the merfolk made up the rhyme to help them remember that Taran's rule can't last forever. I'll read it to you.'

Kes listened carefully as she recited the rhyme aloud.

'Red is the sunrise, Orange the sky,
Golden the shimmering sand.
Green are the pools where the small fishes lie;
Blue water rolls to the land.
Indigo shadows hide secrets in caves;

Violet the glow of the night.
But Silver and Black will call them all back
When a terrible wrong is put right.'

There was silence for a few moments when she finished. Then Kes said, 'Those rainbow colours – they're the colours of the pearls in Taran's crown. And the mirrors in her cave . . .'

'Mirrors?'

'You haven't seen them; you wouldn't know – they're gateways; she can use them to reach different places. That last bit, though . . . "Silver and Black will call them all back" . . . No wonder Taran wants those two pearls so much! The rhyme says it – they're the most powerful ones of all!'

'And we've got them both,' said Lizzy softly.

Kes let out a sharp, whistling breath between clenched teeth. 'Taran knows you've got the silver pearl, but she doesn't know that Father's come back with the black one. Whatever happens, she mustn't find out.' Suddenly he scrambled to his feet. 'Where is Father? I've got to see him – and we have to tell him what's happened!'

'We can't,' Lizzy said in distress. 'He's not here – he went out with Mr Treleaven on his fishing boat this morning. They won't be back till tomorrow or the day after.'

Kes's face fell, and Lizzy felt a surge of sympathy. He was as desperate to meet Jack as she had been; and now there was an even greater urgency.

'I could go and find them,' he said eagerly.

'That's crazy!' Lizzy argued. 'They'll be miles away by now, and you're too tired. Anyway,' she added, 'what about Mr Treleaven and Paul? If you suddenly appear by their boat, in the middle of nowhere –'

Kes sighed. 'I see what you mean.'

'We'll just have to wait till they get back.'

'I suppose so. And in the meantime . . . Look, Lizzy, Mother won't want us to give Taran the silver pearl. But if it's the only way to save her –'

'I don't care about the pearl!' Lizzy said

instantly. 'Mother's safety is the only thing that matters.'

'Then you'll give it to Taran, if we have to?'

'Of course! How could you think I'd do anything else?' Kes sighed with relief, and she added, 'Father would say the same if he were here. I know he would.'

'Waiting's going to be awful. I want to see him so much.' Kes hugged himself as if he were cold. 'What'll we do till he comes back? I'll ask Arhans to watch for the boat; if I go back home she'll tell me when she knows it's coming back. But what about you?'

'I'll just have to carry on as usual, and try to pretend everything's normal.' Lizzy stood up and turned to look inland. 'There are some people coming up the path — I'd better go. Look, can we meet up at the beach later?'

Kes hesitated, then said, 'I don't think we should. Until Father gets here, I think it'd be better — safer — if we stay out of sight. Just in case.'

Lizzy didn't want to agree, but realized that he was right. Tullor, or another creature like him, might easily be lurking and watching. And the less they had to report back to Taran, the better.

'OK,' she said reluctantly. 'But how will I know when Arhans has seen the boat coming home?'

'Listen to your shell,' he told her with a smile. 'When I call, come to the beach then.'

He had given her a large and beautiful spiral shell, which she kept in her room. If she held it to her ear, it echoed the sounds of the sea – but, more than that, she could also hear the strange language of the dolphins and, if Kes called to her, she would be aware of it.

'Yes – yes, I'll do that!' She hugged him quickly and fiercely. 'Take care.'

'I will. See you soon.'

She watched as he slithered a short way down the cliff. For a moment he stood poised, then he launched himself into the air. His body stretched, hands and feet pointing to their full extent, and he soared upwards and outwards in a breathtaking arc before plunging into the sea. Surfacing, he waved to her before turning and vanishing under the water.

Lizzy stood for a minute staring at the tide surging against the cliff base. Then she stepped back from the edge and turned on to the path in the direction of the town. The people she had seen were walking the other way, towards the harbour. They hadn't noticed her and Kes, or, if they had, they hadn't seen Kes disappear.

But someone else had.

'Lizzy?'

Lizzy jumped as Rose appeared in front of her.

'Oh!' She felt the colour draining from her face and tried to hide her dismay under a show of anger. 'What are you *doing*, jumping out at me like that? I thought you were going to watch for the dolphin.'

'And I thought you were going home,' Rose retorted, looking at her sister curiously. 'That was Kes at the lighthouse with you, wasn't it?'

'What if it was?'

'All right, all right; no big deal!' Rose had been on her way back from the harbour when she'd seen Lizzy and Kes together talking very earnestly. She wasn't close enough to hear what they were saying, but it looked important, and that, combined with Lizzy's recent weird moods, had made her want to know what was going on.

Lizzy started to walk on, and Rose followed.

'So what's so deadly secret between you two?' she asked bluntly.

'Don't be stupid.' Lizzy didn't look round. 'There isn't any secret.'

'Then why do you have to sneak up here to talk? Come on, Lizzy: something's up with you, I know it is. We're supposed to be friends, so why won't you tell me?'

Lizzy drew a deep breath, fighting her emotions. She would have given so much to be able to confide in Rose. They had always been close and shared each other's troubles. But this time, for the first time, it wasn't possible. That upset her, and so, though she didn't want to, she lost her temper.

'Just leave me alone, will you?' she snapped. 'There's nothing wrong and, even if there was, it wouldn't be any of your business! All right?'

And before Rose could say any more, she ran on along the path.

Rose stared after her, perplexed. Why did Lizzy keep biting her head off this morning? The first time, at the harbour, Rose had been annoyed, but now she was starting to feel worried. Something *was* up, no doubt of it. And that boy Kes was involved too.

She looked back at the lighthouse and frowned. Where had Kes gone? He hadn't come this way, and she hadn't seen him go towards the harbour, either. Was he still up here, waiting for her to go so that she couldn't ask him any awkward questions?

Well, she thought, *we'll see about that.* Moving quietly, she hurried back to the lighthouse, walked round it to the seaward side, then right round.

Kes wasn't there.

So where had he gone? Rose peered over the

edge of the cliff, thinking that there might be a lower path. But there was only the rocky drop to the sea, and hastily she drew back as it made her feel dizzy. How on earth had Kes managed to get away without her noticing? Anyone would think he'd dived off the cliff and swum away!

She laughed to herself at the craziness of that thought. But she was still baffled as she gave up and started to follow Lizzy back home.

Chapter Three

Morvyr had been dreaming that she was swimming through the oar-weed forest near her cave home. She was looking for something, but when she tried to remember what it was, her mind was strangely blank. The forest seemed to be denser than it should be; when she pushed against the weed strands they pushed back, and she had to fight to make any progress. Then suddenly she couldn't move at all. The oar-weed was pressing in on her, strangling, choking –

She woke with a start, to find herself bathed in a strange, dim indigo light.

Where was she? Her head ached and her

thoughts were vague, but deep down there was a nagging feeling of danger. Had something happened? She couldn't remember . . .

She rolled over in the water and stared around. The indigo light wasn't just dim but seemed dense too, the water thick and sluggish, like the seabed when a current churned up the sand. Then, as her head at last began to clear, her memory came back. Jack – he was back, and she and Kes had left their hideaway at dead of night to find him. They had thought they would be safe – but Tullor and his sidekicks had captured them!

'Kes!' Morvyr cried in distress. 'Kes, are you here?'

Her voice echoed back as though she were in a confined space, but there was no reply. The water swirled as anxiously she started to search in the gloom. She had only gone a metre or two when her outstretched hands met a solid wall and, when she explored it, she found that it curved round her in all directions, so that she was trapped in a small cave-like space.

Quickly she turned right round, and saw that a part of the curving wall was glassy, like the surface of a mirror. In that moment she realized where she was. This was the cave of the rainbow pool, and she was behind one of the mirrors!

Morvyr had visited the rainbow pool many years ago, when the old mermaid Queen, Kara, was alive. Then it had been a happy and delightful place; now, though, it was Taran's lair. Tullor must have brought her here. But why? And where was Kes?

She called Kes's name again. Still no one answered – but suddenly she heard something else. It sounded like laughter. Morvyr swam to the glassy wall and pressed her face against it, peering through.

The scene on the far side was blurry, but she could make out the pool and the other mirrors, glowing with the different colours of the rainbow. On the rock couch at the pool's edge sat Taran herself. She was wearing the circlet of pearls, and in one hand she held up a small looking glass with an ornate gold rim, in which she was admiring her reflection. Morvyr felt a surge of anger. She had seen the looking glass before. The merfolk had found it many years ago, after the wreck of a great sailing-ship, and had given it as a gift to Queen Kara.

'*Thief!*' she whispered bitterly. '*Thief, usurper! What have you done with my son?*'

Taran did not hear her; sound carried only one way through the mirror, it seemed. Then, as Morvyr watched, the water of the pool stirred suddenly and the ugly head of a giant conger eel rose above the surface.

Taran put down the looking glass. 'Ah, Tullor,' she said. 'Is your task completed?'

Tullor writhed; it was his way of bowing. 'Yes, Your Majesty,' he said. 'The boy has gone, and will take your message to his sister.'

Morvyr gasped. Gone? A message to his sister? They must have set Kes free . . . But what was the message? What did Taran want with Lizzy?

Taran tossed her black hair and leaned back

more comfortably on the rock. 'Excellent! Now all we need to do is wait for them to bring us the silver pearl.'

Morvyr froze, hardly able to believe what she was hearing. Taran must have found out that Lizzy had the pearl. But how? Had she forced Kes to tell her? He and Lizzy wouldn't bring her the pearl! They couldn't, they *mustn't* –

Taran was speaking again, and she strained to listen.

'Eight pearls,' the Queen said with satisfaction, 'and then there will only be one more to find.'

'You will find it, Majesty!' Tullor assured her, fawning. 'You are wiser and more cunning than anyone – once you have the silver pearl, the black one can't escape you for long!'

She laughed with pleasure. 'That's true! And when I *do* have the black pearl, I'll make sure everyone in my realm knows about it.' She paused, then a cruel smile spread across her face. 'And I mean *everyone*.'

As she said that, she turned her head and

looked towards the indigo mirror. Luckily Morvyr
was quick-witted enough to close her eyes and
relax, so Taran was fooled into thinking she was
drifting in the water and still asleep.

'And will that include your *other* prisoner,
madam?' Tullor asked.

'Oh, yes,' said Taran darkly. 'I hate her as much
as she hates me, and she knows it. When the
crown is whole again, I will bring her from her
prison and let her witness my triumph.'

Tullor laughed too, though it came out as an
ugly hiss. 'That will be a splendid joke, madam!
When Karwynna sees you wearing the crown, she
will not dare to claim that you are anything but
the true Queen!'

Karwynna? Morvyr drew in a sharp, shocked
breath and dared to open her eyes a fraction.
Taran had stopped looking at her and was
admiring her own reflection again.

'I've been waiting for years to see her face when
I show her the restored crown – *my* crown,' she
said. 'I will take great pleasure in that. And, when

it's done, I can see no reason to keep her alive any longer.'

'Ah, madam,' Tullor was almost crooning, 'then it would be *my* pleasure to deal with her once and for all!'

Taran smiled at him. 'So you shall, Tullor. It will be a reward for your loyalty.'

'*Thank* you, Your Majesty!' There was horrible anticipation in the eel's tone.

'I will rest now,' Taran said. 'Go and watch for the boy and his sister, and bring word to me as soon as they return.'

'As Your Majesty wishes.' Tullor lowered his head and his body writhed. Then he sank beneath the pool's surface and disappeared.

Motionless in her watery cell, Morvyr watched as Taran gave a satisfied sigh and lay back on the rock couch. The Queen's eyes closed, and soon she was asleep. Still Morvyr didn't move, but her mind was whirling with the shock of what she had overheard. She remembered the terrible time when Taran had launched her plot to overthrow the rightful Queen, Kara. Her attack had taken Kara and her servants by surprise; Kara was killed, and Taran had snatched her daughter and heir, Karwynna. For years the merfolk believed that Karwynna must be dead too. Now, though, Morvyr knew that they were wrong. Karwynna was still alive.

But if Taran succeeded in getting her hands on the two missing pearls, Karwynna *would* die.

Tears welled in Morvyr's eyes and mingled with the water in which she swam. It seemed that Taran now had a plan to make Kes and Lizzy bring her the silver pearl. That must not happen! But how could she stop it? She was helpless; she couldn't reach the twins or Arhans, couldn't warn anyone! All she could do was wait, and hope against hope that Taran's plan would fail.

And waiting would be the hardest thing of all.

Chapter Four

'Well, you really are a talkative pair,' Mum said when the Baxters were having supper that evening. 'We've hardly had a word out of either of you.' She looked shrewdly from Rose to Lizzy. 'Are you both feeling all right?'

Lizzy looked up. 'What? Er – yes, fine, Mum. I just . . . haven't got anything to talk about.'

'Me neither,' said Rose.

Dad, who never missed a chance to tease, said, 'Missing Paul already, Rose? Ah, young love!' He winked at Mum, who made a mock swipe at him with her fork.

'Shut up, Dad,' said Rose. 'Anyway, they'll probably be back tomorrow.'

Lizzy looked up quickly. 'Do you know? Has Paul texted you?'

She was pretending to be casual, but Rose wasn't fooled. 'What's with the big interest all of a sudden?' she asked curiously. 'Wanting to see them off, and now wanting to know when they'll be back. What are you up to?'

'Nothing. Don't be stupid!'

'Lizzy!' Mum said sharply. 'That's enough! You too, Rose. If you want to argue with each other, do it somewhere else.'

Both girls fell silent. Rose had been about to ask Lizzy bluntly what she and Kes had been talking about so secretively at the lighthouse, and how Kes had managed to disappear so quickly and completely. Now, though, she was glad Mum had stopped her in time. Something *was* going on, she was certain. But, if she pushed, Lizzy would just clam up and say nothing. If she was going to get some answers,

Rose told herself, there were better ways to do it.

The meal was finished in awkward silence, and as soon as she was allowed to Lizzy left the room. Rose heard her going upstairs, then the sound of her bedroom door opening. Sulking, probably, she decided. But as she helped clear the table Lizzy came down the stairs again. She didn't say anything, didn't even look at Rose, but joined in to do her share of the clearing and washing up.

Now, this really *was* strange, Rose thought. All day Lizzy had repeatedly disappeared up to her room. She never stayed there for more than a few minutes, but she kept on doing it, and Rose couldn't work out why. Was she phoning someone on her mobile? And, if so, who was it? If – or when – she did it again, it might be worth trying to find out.

The chance came when the washing up was done and Dad was drying the last of the plates. Rose saw Lizzy slip away and up the stairs, and after a few seconds she went after her.

Lizzy's door was ajar, and Rose expected to

hear her talking on her mobile. But there was no sound from inside the room. Doubly curious now, Rose tiptoed to the door and cautiously put her eye to the narrow gap.

Lizzy was standing by the window. She had picked up the big spiral shell that she'd brought home from the beach a couple of weeks ago, and she was holding it to her ear. Rose was baffled. Was *that* why Lizzy kept coming up here? It wasn't just strange, it was downright weird! And there was such a look of concentration on Lizzy's face. Was she pretending the shell was a phone? She must have gone completely nuts!

Suddenly Lizzy lowered the shell and put it down on the window ledge. She turned, and Rose dashed along the landing to the bathroom before her sister could emerge and see her. She was only just in time. But, peering round the bathroom door, she saw the deep frown on Lizzy's face as she went back downstairs.

Rose was no nearer to solving the mystery by bedtime, and the following day Lizzy seemed

more distracted than ever. She still repeatedly
went to her room, though Rose didn't risk
following her again in case she should be caught.

Lizzy, though, was completely uninterested in
Rose. As the day went on and there was no signal
from Kes, she grew more and more tense. How
much longer would she have to wait? Where was
the *Regard*? Had anything gone wrong?

Then, just before teatime, she picked up the
shell yet again and heard, among the rushing sea
sounds, Kes's voice.

'*Lizzy . . . Lizzy . . . The harbour. Dusk. The
harbour . . .*'

Lizzy's heart leaped with excitement and relief.
This must mean that the trawler was coming in!
She rushed downstairs and almost cannoned into
Rose, who was reading a text on her mobile and
not looking where she was going.

'Careful!' Rose said, flailing her arms to regain
her balance.

'Sorry.' Then Lizzy stopped, staring at the phone
in her sister's hand. 'What are you reading? A text?'

'Yeah.'

'Who's it from?'

Rose gave her a sharp look. 'None of your business,' she said, and walked away. Lizzy stared after her. Was the text from Paul? Was the boat back in mobile range, and had he told Rose when they would arrive? She ached to ask but didn't dare; it would look too obvious. She would just have to wait a while longer.

Mr and Mrs Baxter were going out that evening. A film they wanted to see was showing in Penzance and Mrs Baxter said that she couldn't remember the last time they had been to the cinema together, and alone.

'Last time, we had to get a babysitter for you two,' she told the girls. 'It must have been years ago! I'm so glad that Rose is old enough now to look after Lizzy.'

Rose raised her eyes heavenward in mock despair, and Lizzy said indignantly, 'I'm old enough to look after myself!'

'Maybe, but I still wouldn't leave you at home

alone all evening. So, no going out tonight, Rose, all right?'

'All right,' Rose said with a long-suffering air. 'Anyway, I wasn't planning to. Paul's getting back soon, but he says he's too tired to see me tonight.' She shrugged. 'So I might as well be stuck here as anywhere else.'

Paul's getting back . . . So Rose's text *was* from him. It was the confirmation Lizzy had been hoping for, and she felt herself relax. Just a few more hours, that was all.

When their parents had gone, Rose flopped down in front of the TV. For a while Lizzy sat with her, trying to distract herself by staring at the screen. But she was nervous and fidgety, so as soon as it was late enough not to arouse suspicion she stood up, stretched her arms very obviously and said, 'I'm going to bed. 'Night, Rose.'

Rose apparently wasn't concentrating. 'Yeah,' she said vaguely. ''Night.'

Upstairs in her room Lizzy waited impatiently for dusk. At last the sun flared down behind the house and shadows in the streets and harbour merged into grey. She couldn't bear to delay any longer and, pulling on a jumper, she tiptoed down the stairs and peered warily into the sitting room. Rose was sprawled on the sofa, punching out a text on her mobile. The TV was still on but with the sound turned down, and Rose was now listening to music on her iPod. Relieved, Lizzy backed away and went through the kitchen and out by the back door. There was a little alleyway behind the garden gate, and from there she could get round to the street. It was safer and quieter than using the front entrance.

She closed the door with a gentle click and hurried away.

In the house, Rose sat up and looked thoughtfully towards the hall. Her busy-ness had been a pretence. She had heard Lizzy creeping downstairs and seen her peeking round the door, and when she vanished again Rose took out the earpiece of her iPod (which wasn't switched on anyway) and listened carefully. Then she'd heard the back door open and shut. OK; as she had expected, Lizzy was up to something. So maybe now she really could find out what it was.

Lizzy did not look back as she hastened on to the harbour, but, if she had, she might have glimpsed a shadowy figure following her cautiously along the street.

The harbour was quiet. A few evening sightseers were strolling about, and Lizzy stopped on the quay and gazed over the scene. The last reflections of light on the sea were fading as darkness crept across the bay, and there seemed to be no activity around the fishing boats. For a few moments she wondered if she had arrived too early. But Kes had said dusk . . . Then suddenly she saw two familiar figures, one tall and the other much smaller, on the quay wall. Jack and Kes were there!

She ran to them. 'You've found each other – oh, I'm so *glad*!'

'So am I.' Jack's eyes were misty with emotion. 'Now I've got both my children back at long last!'

Kes, too, was shiny-eyed; even his fear for
Morvyr couldn't dim the joy of being reunited
with his father. But, after the first happiness and
excitement, they all sobered as they started to talk
about what they should do.

Kes had already repeated his story to Jack, and
to the twins' relief Jack felt the same way as they
did.

'We've got to give Taran the pearl,' he said. 'I
hate the thought of it, but there's no other choice.
Rescuing Morvyr is more important than anything
else.'

Kes frowned. 'But will she keep her promise
and set Mother free? I don't trust her.'

'Neither do I,' Lizzy agreed.

Jack sighed. 'We can't be sure, of course. But I
don't think she'll cheat us. She knows that Morvyr
hasn't got the black pearl, so what's the point in
keeping her prisoner? And once you've given her
the silver pearl you two are no more use to her
either.'

'I suppose so,' Kes said reluctantly. 'But I'm

still scared.' He glanced at his sister. 'And I don't like the idea of Lizzy having to come too. We've got to take the pearl through its own special gateway, so that Taran will know it's not a fake. The gateway's far out past Land's End; Arhans told me. Even if the dolphins help, it's a very long way for Lizzy to swim. But Taran said she has to bring it herself.'

'Mmm . . .' Jack stroked his chin thoughtfully. 'I might have an answer to that. Kes, if I took Lizzy to the gateway by boat, do you think Arhans and her friends would show us the way?'

Kes's face lit up. 'Yes, I'm sure they would! And it'd be great if you were with us, Father – I'd feel so much safer!'

'Me too,' Lizzy added; then her smile faded. 'But if you mean Mr Treleaven's boat, it's very small. *Could* you take it a long way out to sea?'

'I'm not talking about his sailing-boat,' said Jack. 'I'm talking about *Regard*.'

She stared at him. 'The trawler? What about

Mr Treleaven, though? He'd have to come too, wouldn't he?'

'Yes, he would.' Jack's eyes met hers, very steadily. 'I know what you're thinking, but you needn't worry. Jeff has always been a good friend of mine. A *very* good friend.'

'You mean . . .' Her eyes widened. 'He *knows*?'

Jack smiled and put a finger to his lips. 'I'm not saying what he does or doesn't know. Just trust me. All right?'

'All right,' said Lizzy dubiously.

'That's my girl. Then all I have to do is persuade Jeff to invite you out on a little day-trip. Do you think your parents will agree, if he rings them tomorrow?' She nodded. 'Good. Then you'd better get on home, before anyone misses you. I'll get everything fixed up as soon as I can. And when we go out don't forget your wetsuit!'

Lizzy hurried back through the dark streets with her mind whirling. From what Jack had said, it seemed that Mr Treleaven knew and accepted the truth about his past, or at least some of it. But how much? For instance, did he know that she and Kes were Jack's children? Or about Morvyr? Or the black and silver pearls? It was strange and wonderful to think that someone else might share their secret and, what was more, believe it.

Reaching the alley that ran behind her house, she turned into it and headed towards the back garden gate. Rose, who was just a few metres behind her, had counted on that, and quickly she let herself in at the front door. When Lizzy crept from the kitchen to the hall and peeked round the half-open door, she saw her sister still sprawled on the sofa with her earphones on, apparently fast asleep. Smiling with relief, Lizzy glided noiselessly up the stairs and to her bedroom.

While, downstairs, Rose opened her eyes and stared at the wall without seeing it. She had a great deal to think about. A very great deal indeed.

Chapter Five

The next day Mr Baxter went to the college where he was to start teaching next month, to talk with the Head of Department about the coming year's curriculum. While he was 'out of the way', as she put it, Mrs Baxter decided to redecorate their bedroom, which was painted a ghastly shade of pinky-beige. To her surprise, Lizzy offered to help.

'Aren't you going to the beach?' Mum said. 'It's another lovely day; surely you don't want to be stuck indoors?'

'I don't mind,' said Lizzy. 'Honest, Mum, I'd like to help.'

'Well, I'm not going to turn down an offer like that!' Mum grinned at her. 'Come on, then. But wear something that you don't mind getting painty.'

In old shorts and T-shirts they had soon shifted the bedroom furniture and were at work washing down the walls. Lizzy was thankful that Rose was out with Paul. Her sister had been asking a lot of curious questions lately, and this readiness to stay at home would have made her very suspicious. The truth was that Lizzy didn't want to go anywhere until Mr Treleaven phoned about the boat trip. There was no guarantee, of course, that he would agree to Jack's idea. But, if he did, Lizzy wanted to be here when he rang Mum to talk about it.

They were washing the last wall when the phone shrilled loudly. Lizzy nearly jumped out of her skin, but luckily Mum didn't notice and picked up the bedroom extension.

'Hi, Janice,' she said. 'Yes, fine, thanks – and you?'

Lizzy let out her breath with a rush. It was Mum's friend from the hospital where she worked part time. Mum chatted for a minute or so, then said, 'Yes, I'll be there. Thanks. Bye,' and hung up.

'Someone in the department's off sick, so they want me for an extra day this week,' she said as she picked up her sponge again.

'Oh, right.' Lizzy didn't know what else to say, and put extra energy into the washing. They left the walls to dry for half an hour, with the window wide open, then it was time to start on the painting. The phone didn't ring again, and Lizzy tried not to think about it, but to concentrate instead on telling herself how nice the new light sea-blue colour was going to look.

They broke for lunch, which was ham and salad and coleslaw. As they were finishing it, and Mum was saying how much faster the bedroom was coming on with two of them working, the phone *did* ring. Again Lizzy jumped, but Mum still didn't notice.

'Hello?' she said into the receiver. Then: 'Oh, hello, Mr Treleaven.'

Lizzy's heart missed a beat so violently that it hurt. *This is it*, she thought.

'On your boat? . . . Tomorrow? Well, the only thing is, how long were you planning to go for? . . . Oh, I see; just a day-trip . . . Yes, of course; I don't see why not. I'm sure they'll both love it.'

Lizzy froze. *Both?* What did she mean, *both*?

'Lizzy's here now,' Mum went on. 'Rose is out, but as soon as she comes in . . . Oh, of course, Paul's already told her. Well, that's very kind of you, Mr Treleaven. And very exciting for the girls! We'll speak later – goodbye.'

She turned to Lizzy with a broad smile. 'You've got an invitation,' she said, 'to go out for a day-trip on Mr Treleaven's boat tomorrow.'

'Oh . . .' Lizzy tried her best to look surprised. 'That's . . . wonderful.'

'Well, I must say you don't sound very pleased,' said Mum. 'I thought you'd be thrilled.'

Hastily Lizzy pulled herself together. 'I am,

Mum, really – it's great! I just – didn't expect it.'
She hesitated. 'Did he say Rose as well?'

'Of course! Paul's her boyfriend, so she's hardly
going to be left out, is she? You'll have to make
sure you've both got warm clothes and life jackets.
And I'll do you packed lunches, all right?'

'Yes . . . thanks, Mum.' She forced her face into
a happy expression. 'It'll be . . . brilliant.'

All afternoon Lizzy worked furiously at the
decorating. She was trying to take her mind off
the disastrous setback, but she couldn't stop
worrying about it. If Rose was with them on the
trawler, how on earth could they carry out their
plan? Everything could be ruined. There *had* to be
a way to stop Rose from coming!

The trouble was she couldn't think of anything
that would work. She had plenty of ideas, but they
got wilder and wilder as the day went on. And
when she reached the point of thinking that
perhaps she could creep into Rose's room tonight
and paint measles spots on her face and neck,

Lizzy admitted defeat. Her only hope was that Rose wouldn't want to go.

But when Rose came home the hope was dashed. Rose was bubbling with enthusiasm about the trip. And as she talked about it she kept giving Lizzy a look of pure triumph. Lizzy didn't understand why. However, she soon found out when she followed Rose to her room, hoping that she might be able to persuade her to change her mind.

Rose was checking her emails, but when Lizzy came in she turned away from the computer and said, 'Ah. I thought you'd come up here soon.'

Lizzy didn't know what she meant, so she ignored the remark. 'Look, Rose,' she said awkwardly, 'I was just wondering . . . well, going out on a trawler's not going to be like going on a pleasure-boat, is it? It'll be really noisy, and not very comfortable, and everything'll stink of fish and things. And the sea's sure to be much rougher when we get a long way out. So I sort of thought . . .'

'Oh,' said Rose, looking innocent and pretending to misunderstand, 'you mean, you don't really want to go?'

'No! Not me. I was thinking about you.'

A grin spread slowly across Rose's face. 'Yes,' she said, 'I know you were. And I know why.'

Lizzy stared, dismayed.

'You see,' Rose went on, 'I followed you to the harbour last night.'

The colour drained from Lizzy's face. 'What?'

'Come on – don't try to fool me. I followed you, and I saw you meet Mr Carrick and that boy Kes. You're up to something, Lizzy Baxter – I've known it for days, and it's howlingly obvious that this trawler trip's got something to do with it.' She studied Lizzy's horrified expression and her suspicions were confirmed. 'I want in on the secret, so there's no *way* you're going to stop me from coming. If you try, I'll tell Mum and Dad what happened last night, and then you won't be allowed to go at all!'

In that awful moment Lizzy realized that she

was cornered. Rose wouldn't believe the truth, even if she could have found the words to tell her. Making up a convincing story on the spot was impossible too. So she had only one choice.

She sank on to the edge of Rose's bed and stared down at her own feet. 'Look,' she said, 'there *is* a secret, and it's desperately important to me. But I've promised that I won't tell anyone. Not even you.' She looked up, her eyes pleading. 'I want to, but . . . I promised faithfully. When it's sorted out, I'll be able to explain everything. For now, though . . . *Please*, Rose, don't tell Mum and Dad about yesterday. And don't try to make me tell you any more!'

Rose and Lizzy were good friends and Rose didn't want to make trouble for her sister. Besides, she reminded herself, if she gave Lizzy away she would never find out what the secret was.

'Just tell me one thing,' she said. 'This isn't dangerous or anything, is it? For you, I mean?'

Lizzy knew that if Rose tried for a hundred

years she would never guess just how dangerous it was. But though she hated lying, she had to do it.

'No,' she replied. 'It's OK. Honestly it is.'

'Well . . .' Rose sighed. 'All right, then. I won't tell anyone, and I won't ask you any more questions. But,' she grinned suddenly, 'I'm still coming on that boat trip!'

Chapter Six

The girls were to be at the harbour at eight
o'clock the next morning. Lizzy got up at six.
Excitement and nerves were fighting each other,
and her stomach felt as if it were full of little
turning wheels. She had lain awake most of the
night, worrying about how she and Kes could
carry out their plan to take the pearl to Taran
with Rose on board the boat, but she'd not come
up with any answers. She could only hope that
Jack would think of something. Either that, or
Rose would change her mind at the last minute
and stay behind.

The hope was dashed when she tried to get

into the bathroom and discovered that Rose was already there.

'Won't be long!' Rose sang out over the noise of the shower splashing. 'Isn't it a gorgeous day? I can't wait to get out on the sea!'

Mum had got up too when she heard the girls, and by the time Lizzy had showered she was cooking breakfast for them.

'You don't want to go off on empty stomachs,' she said. 'And I'm doing you packed lunches too.'

'Great; thanks, Mum,' said Rose. She ate ravenously when the breakfast was ready, but Lizzy had to force herself to finish every mouthful. Her locket, with the silver pearl inside, was on its chain round her neck, and every few moments she touched it as though to make sure that it hadn't suddenly vanished into nowhere.

By quarter to eight Rose was impatient to go.

'Have you got everything?' Mum asked.

'Sure!' Rose slapped her shoulder-bag. 'Camera, sunglasses, factor thirty suncream – and my bikini's on under my shorts, for sunbathing.'

'We're going on a trawler, not on a cruise,' said Lizzy sharply.

'So? I'll find somewhere to stretch out in the sun, you watch me!' Rose grinned. 'Bye, Mum – see you later!'

She hurried out of the front door. Lizzy made to follow, then suddenly, on impulse, turned back and hugged Mrs Baxter with all her strength. 'Bye, Mum!'

Mum looked surprised and pleased. She waved as the girls headed off down the street, then closed the door, wondering why Lizzy had hugged her so hard.

Rose had noticed too, and as soon as they were out of Mum's earshot she said, 'What was that for?'

'What?'

'That huge hug you gave Mum.'

'Nothing,' Lizzy replied defensively. 'I just felt like it.'

Rose looked disbelieving. She was curious about something else too. 'And why have you got your *wetsuit* on under your clothes? That's nuts!'

Lizzy flushed. 'No, it isn't. It can get cold on the sea.'

Rose opened her mouth to ask another question, but something made her change her mind. As she had told herself last night, if she pushed Lizzy too hard, she wouldn't learn anything at all. So she just said, 'OK. Your choice.'

Lizzy breathed a sigh of relief.

The fish market was nearly over, but the dockside was still bustling with activity. The girls couldn't pick out the *Regard* from among all the other boats, but then Rose saw someone waving to them from further along the harbour.

'There's Paul!' She waved back and broke into a run, Lizzy on her heels. They dodged a trundling forklift truck and two men pushing a trolley loaded with empty boxes, and there, too, were Mr Treleaven and Jack waiting to meet them. Jack gave Lizzy a very special look but only said cheerfully, 'Morning, girls! You made it, then?'

'Of course we did, Mr Carrick!' Rose pretended

to be indignant, though she was smiling at him. 'Are you coming with us?'

'Oh, yes. You can't keep an old fisherman away from the sea, you know.'

Rose went towards the boat with Paul and his father, but Jack hung back and whispered, 'I'm sorry, Lizzy, but there was nothing I could do. It would have looked strange if we'd invited you but not Rose, wouldn't it?'

Lizzy nodded. 'I know. But how are we going to do what we need to, without her knowing?'

'We'll have to distract her somehow. I've got a few ideas, but we can talk about that once we're at sea. For now, just pretend that everything's fine, OK?'

'I'll try. But she already knows something's going on.' Lizzy told him what had happened last night, about her confession and Rose's promise.

Jack frowned. 'Will she keep the promise, do you think?'

Lizzy hesitated, then replied, 'Yes. I'm sure she will. But she's busting to know the secret.'

'Well, that's another problem we must solve when we have to. It's a pity she followed you, but you mustn't blame yourself; you weren't to know. We'll sort it out, Lizzy, don't worry. Now, Arhans isn't far away. When she sees the boat leave, she'll fetch Kes and they'll follow us.' Briefly and reassuringly he squeezed her hand. 'Come on. Let's get aboard before the others wonder what we're up to.'

Regard left her mooring twenty minutes later, easing out stern first and then turning slowly until her bows pointed to the sea. As she glided towards the harbour entrance Lizzy stood by the wheelhouse, watching the quay slip past. She had never been on a boat of this size before; it was a completely new experience and it was fascinating. There was the rough chug-chugging of the trawler's engine, the vibration of the deck under her feet, and the rhythmic dip and rise of their movement, like a huge, gentle rocking chair. She could smell the sea, but there were other smells too: diesel and oil and fish and others she didn't recognize, all mixing together.

Rose came to join her, pushing back her dark hair that the wind blew around her face. 'Great, isn't it?' she said. 'Except for this wretched thing . . .' She wriggled her shoulders, trying to adjust the life jacket she had been made to put on. 'I won't get much of a tan through this!'

'You won't get drowned if you fall overboard, either,' Lizzy pointed out. Jack had told her to wear a jacket too; they both knew she didn't need it, but they had to keep up appearances.

Rose raised her eyebrows. 'I've no intention of falling overboard, thanks! The sea's much too cold. Though you with that wetsuit –'

'Oh, don't start that again! I told you why I'm wearing it.'

Rose opened her mouth, hesitated, then thought better of what she had been going to say and changed the subject. 'Paul says we're going right out past Land's End. I wonder if we'll see any dolphins?'

The remark sounded casual, but Lizzy knew Rose was watching her for some kind of reaction, so she just smiled and didn't answer. They had reached the end of the quay wall now, and as the boat turned towards the open sea the rocking motion suddenly became stronger.

'Whoops!' Rose swayed and staggered and nearly tripped over a metal bar that projected up from the deck. 'I hope it isn't going to be rough!'

'This isn't rough,' said Lizzy. 'You wait till we get further out.' Then, realizing that she wasn't supposed to know about that sort of thing, she added quickly, 'Remember when we went on that Sea Safari, when we first came here? The guy who took us said it was a calm day, but it was much lumpier than this.'

'Yes, it was, wasn't it?' Rose pulled a face. 'Oh, well; if I get seasick, I get seasick.'

'You'll be OK,' said Paul, coming up behind them. 'I'm making tea in a minute. Fisherman's tea cures anything!'

He was probably right, Lizzy thought a short

while later, looking dubiously at the steaming mug that was put into her hand. The tea was the colour of very old bricks, and when she cautiously sipped it even the three spoonfuls of sugar that Paul had put in couldn't hide the overpowering taste.

'Yuk!' Rose whispered. 'This is dis*gust*ing! How can anyone say they actually *like* it?' She glanced furtively over her shoulder to make sure Paul wasn't nearby. 'I'm going to chuck mine overboard when no one's looking!'

'Me too.' Lizzy grinned. She wondered where Arhans and Kes were now. They might already be following the boat, and she had a sudden vision of the tea sploshing into the sea where Kes was swimming, and what he would think of the taste. That made her start to giggle, and Rose stared at her.

'It wasn't *that* funny,' she said.

'Sorry.' Lizzy knew that the giggling fit was a result of nerves, and she forced herself to stop. Where *were* Kes and Arhans? Surreptitiously she

looked over the rail to the sea below. But the
water was churning with the wash from the
Regard's bows, and it was impossible to see
anything below the surface. Wondering if Jack was
looking too, she raised her head again and
glanced around. But Jack was with Mr Treleaven
in the wheelhouse; she could see them through
the window, talking and laughing together. She
sighed inwardly. She should try to be like him and
stop worrying. They were hardly out of the
harbour yet; there was plenty of time. She must
control her impatience, and wait.

Chapter Seven

By the time the dramatic cliffs of Land's End slid by on their right-hand side – which Lizzy had now learned to call the starboard beam – there was still no sign of Kes or the dolphins.

Rose had decided to sunbathe, but on the deck of a fishing trawler that was far from easy. She had been grumbling to Lizzy that there simply wasn't any spot where a person could stretch out properly without banging their head, knees or elbows against hatch covers, fishing gear or some bolted-down lump of metal that couldn't be moved out of the way. Eventually she had solved the problem by lying down in a small inflatable boat that was lashed on top of a hatch cover. Paul laughed when he saw her, but now he'd given up teasing and was with Lizzy at the rail.

'See the lighthouse away to starboard?' he said, pointing. 'That's the Longships. At night you can see its light from nearly twenty miles away.'

Lizzy gazed at the distant, lonely tower and smiled. 'It's a bit different from our little one at home!'

'Too right! It's got a helicopter landing-pad on the top – can you just imagine how ours would look with one of those?'

She laughed, then turned to call over her shoulder to Rose. 'Rose, did you hear that? The lighthouse over there has got a helicopter pad on top!'

'Oh. Right,' said Rose. Her voice sounded peculiar, and Lizzy turned round. 'Rose? You OK?'

Rose had sat up but was hunched over her drawn-up knees. Her face had lost its colour, and for a moment she didn't answer. Then she said, 'No. I feel queasy.'

'Uh-oh,' said Paul. 'She's seasick.' He left the

rail and went over to her. 'Come on, Rose, it'll only get worse if you sit here. The best thing is to turn your face to the wind and focus your eyes on the horizon.'

He tried to help her to her feet, but Rose groaned and shook her head. 'No-o-o! I just want to lie down . . .'

'All right. Not here, though. Let's get you below, and you can lie on one of the bunks. Give me a hand with her, Lizzy, yeah?'

Between them they got Rose out of the small boat and helped her towards the companion ladder that led down to the crew's cabin. Jack and Mr Treleaven saw them, and Mr Treleaven came out of the wheelhouse.

'Seasick?' He eyed Rose sympathetically. 'Bad luck, Rose. Give her the centre bunk, Paul; she won't notice the motion of the boat so much there. And give her an anti-nausea tablet if she can take it; they're in the first-aid box.' He paused, then smiled with wry humour. 'And you'd better make sure she's got a bucket handy.'

'Don't wanna tablet or a bucket . . .' Rose mumbled. 'Just wanna *die* . . .'

Somehow Paul and Lizzy got Rose down the ladder to the cabin, where they made her as comfortable as they could. Lizzy felt she ought to sit with her sister, but Paul shook his head.

'She's feeling so lousy she won't notice whether anyone's here or not,' he said. 'If we leave her alone she'll probably sleep, and that'll help. Trust me, I know; it happened to me every trip for six months when I first started fishing with Dad!'

Lizzy admitted to herself that she would much rather go back on deck, and pushed down the thought that she was being mean. Truthfully, Rose's seasickness was an answer to her biggest problem – and she soon found out that Jack agreed.

'Don't feel guilty,' he told her when she emerged through the hatch into the fresh air again. 'It would have happened in any case, and it *does* keep her out of the way.'

'I suppose so.' Lizzy was still having a tussle with her conscience, but tried hard to ignore it. 'Have you seen Kes or the dolphins yet?' she asked, lowering her voice.

He smiled. 'Go up for'ard, and look over the rail.'

Her eyes lit up and she hurried along the deck to the *Regard*'s bows. And there they were – five dolphins leaping and diving as they sped through the sea ahead of the trawler. Lizzy saw Arhans's silver streak as she led them, and her heartbeat quickened with excitement.

'They know where we've got to go,' said Jack, coming to stand beside her. 'All we have to do is follow them.'

Follow them . . . Quickly Lizzy turned to glance at the wheelhouse. Mr Treleaven was at the wheel. His face was unreadable, and she thought: *was* he following the dolphins? What had Jack told him? Could he possibly know about Kes, and what they were planning to do?

She looked at Jack with the question in her

eyes, but, as he had done once before when she'd asked, he only smiled and put a finger to his lips. Then he too turned towards the wheelhouse and nodded to Mr Treleaven. Mr Treleaven nodded in reply, and called out to Paul, who was in the stern checking the fishing gear.

'Paul! Leave that for now, boy; we're not going to shoot the trawl for a while yet. I haven't put the new diaphragm on that bilge pump that's been playing up. Go down and sort it, will you? And stay with it for a while when you've finished, to make sure it's working properly.'

'OK, Dad.' Paul headed for the companion ladder. 'Anyone want more tea?'

'Not now. You'd better check on Rose, though.'

Paul vanished, and Lizzy thought: *So Mr Treleaven does know something.* It was obvious that Paul was being deliberately sent below so that he wouldn't see what was going to happen. She looked at Mr Treleaven again, but his face was as inscrutable as ever as he gazed ahead over the sea and the *Regard* chugged on.

'I haven't seen Kes yet,' Jack said quietly. 'But he's there, you can be sure of it. I think you can tell Arhans that it's safe for him to come to the surface now.'

Lizzy's stomach began to churn. But it wasn't seasickness. Going to the rail, she looked out to where the dolphins were, then raised her hand and waved. Almost at once Arhans turned in the water and swam back towards the boat. Within moments she was gliding alongside, and Lizzy saw her dark, expressive eyes gazing up.

'Arhans!' She leaned over the rail. 'Tell Kes it's clear now – he can come up!'

Arhans whistled, the sound carrying even over the noises of the sea and the *Regard*'s throbbing engine. Then with a graceful flick of her tail she dived and vanished. Lizzy waited, trying not to count the seconds, then Arhans appeared again, with Kes beside her.

'Lizzy!' he shouted, waving eagerly. 'We're nearly at the gateway – are you ready?'

'Yes!' Lizzy called.

'Come on, then!'

'Hold on.' Jack put a hand on Lizzy's arm. 'Wait till the boat slows down.' Again he looked at Mr Treleaven at the wheel, and as if there were some kind of telepathy between them, the skipper reached to the engine controls. The throbbing rhythm changed and quietened, and Lizzy felt the deck vibrate under her feet as the trawler began to lose way. The churning white wash lessened, and Jack touched her arm again.

'All right. Be careful, both of you – and good luck!'

Lizzy was already pulling off her clothes, revealing the wetsuit underneath. She touched the locket, which hung round her neck with the silver pearl safe inside, and her heart began to thump as she thought about what she and Kes must now do. They were so far from land; the sea looked so huge and deep . . . a sudden surge of panic hit her and she thought, *I can't do it! I'm too scared!*

She turned to Jack. 'I wish you were coming too!'

'So do I.' His face was very serious. 'But I can't. We don't want Taran to find out that I've come back. Besides, I'm only an ordinary human, remember. It was Queen Kara's magic that allowed me to live under the sea for a while, like you and Kes. But the magic wore off a long time ago, and only someone with the Queen's power could make it work again.' He smiled sadly. 'I can't imagine Taran being kind enough to do that, can you?'

Slowly Lizzy nodded, and with a great effort squashed her feelings down. She and Kes had to do this alone. And she couldn't let fear get the better of her. For Morvyr's sake . . .

She hugged Jack quickly but tightly. Then she climbed on to the rail, took a deep breath as she balanced there for a moment and dived into the sea.

Jack watched as Lizzy cleaved into the water and vanished. Arhans had dived too, but Kes was still bobbing on the surface. He grinned bravely as Jack gave him a thumbs-up sign, then he too disappeared under the water. Jack stared at the place where they had been, until a voice called to him.

'Jack.' Mr Treleaven had opened the window of the wheelhouse and was leaning out. 'Better get the trawl ready. Got to keep up appearances, eh?'

Jack shook off his uneasy thoughts. 'Right, Jeff,' he said. And with a last glance at the sea he started towards the stern of the boat.

Chapter Eight

The sea was stunningly cold. Lizzy was unprepared for it, and gasped with shock as she plunged downward through the blue-green water. Then she felt Kes's hand on her arm, and turned to see him swimming beside her.

'It's – it's *icy*!' she stammered, bubbles streaming from her mouth.

'I know,' said Kes. 'It's because we're so far from land. Can you stand it? Are you all right?'

'Y-yes . . . I think so. It's just my head and hands, where the wetsuit doesn't cover me . . .' She shuddered, treading water. 'I'll warm up once we s-start swimming properly.'

The dolphins had gathered round them now, and Arhans nudged Lizzy with her blunt snout as though to reassure her.

'We haven't got far to go,' Kes said. 'Come on – let's get going, before I lose my nerve!'

Grasping her hand, he towed her away through the water with a powerful flick of his tail, the dolphins swimming alongside. Lizzy still wasn't quite used to seeing her brother in his merboy form. And stranger still was the thought that, if only she could find a way to turn the forgotten key in her mind, she too could change her shape and be like him. She had tried so hard, but she couldn't make it happen. Right now, to have speed and stamina like Kes's would have given her a lot more confidence.

She tried not to think about that as they surged on through the sea. The currents out here were hugely powerful; Lizzy could feel them pulling at her and was thankful that Kes had a tight hold of her hand. He was leading her down as well as onwards; the light from above was almost gone and they were swimming nearly blind. But Arhans knew exactly where they were going, and before long Lizzy saw the dim outlines of a reef looming in the near-darkness ahead.

The rocks reared up like the fangs of a weird sea monster as they drew closer. Seaweed grew thickly on them, and all kinds of living things scurried among the weed. Lizzy thought she saw a strange, blue-black creature shifting in a crevice, but the dolphins guided her and Kes away from it to a place where the fangs gave way to a large, bowl-shaped hollow in the rock. Arhans nosed at it with her snout, then whistled, and Kes said, 'She says this is it. The silver gateway.'

Lizzy stared dubiously. 'It looks like just any ordinary rock. Is she *sure* this is the right place?'

'Arhans wouldn't have got it wrong.'

'But how do we open it?'

'I don't know.' Kes shivered. 'All Taran told me was that we have to bring the pearl here. Maybe – *oh*!'

His words broke off in a gasp of shock as a

huge black shape loomed out of the darkness. Lizzy stifled a scream as she recognized the long, sinuous body of Tullor, the giant conger eel. The dolphins reacted furiously, but before they could do anything Tullor snarled, 'Get back! I am on Her Majesty's business, and you will not *dare* to touch me!' He turned his cold, evil eyes on Lizzy and Kes, and his mouth gaped open, showing savage teeth in his version of a smile. 'I am here to take you to Queen Taran. Send your interfering friends away – and hurry! Her Majesty does not like to be kept waiting!'

Arhans chittered angrily, but Kes held up a hand to silence her. 'It's all right, Arhans. Lizzy and I have got to do this on our own. You'd better go.' He smiled at the dolphin, trying to look and sound braver than he felt. 'We'll be back soon.'

Arhans and her friends weren't happy, but they didn't argue. Slowly they backed away, then as one they turned and streaked off. As they vanished into the dark, Tullor hissed with satisfaction.

'You are a sensible boy, Kesson. And you, Tegenn.' He looked at Lizzy in a way that made her shudder. 'It pleases me to meet you again. And it will please the Queen even more – if you have brought the silver pearl.'

Mustering her courage, Lizzy forced herself to look steadily at him. 'I've brought it,' she said.

'Good. Then do exactly as I tell you, and I will take you to Her Majesty.' Tullor swam to the dip in the rock and looked back at them. 'Come here,' he commanded.

Lizzy felt Kes's hand squeeze hers as they followed Tullor and drifted above the hollow.

'Take the pearl from its hiding-place, and hold it towards the gateway,' said the eel.

Lizzy hesitated, but Kes said, 'Do it, Lizzy. He won't try to trick us. He's too scared of the Queen.'

Tullor showed his teeth angrily but Lizzy was reassured. She opened the locket that hung round her neck, then gently stroked the inside surface. The secret compartment sprang open, and silvery light spilled through her fingers.

Tullor's eyes glittered greedily. '*Yes!*' he growled. 'Hold it over the gate! Quickly!'

Grasping the pearl, Lizzy stretched out her hand until it was directly above the rock bowl. Immediately an answering silver light came to life at the bottom of the bowl. It merged with the light from the pearl, turning the undersea gloom to brilliance and making Kes and Lizzy look like ghosts. Then suddenly Lizzy felt a squirming sensation under her clenched fingers, as if she were holding something alive.

'Kes, the pearl – it's trying to escape!'

'Hold on to it!' Kes said urgently. 'Whatever happens, don't let go!'

The light was so bright now that Lizzy had to shield her eyes with her free hand. The brightness began to swirl and twist, until it became a silver whirlpool. It caught hold of Lizzy, Kes and Tullor, spinning them round – then Lizzy felt herself being wrenched away and down, turning and turning, arms flailing as she was pulled towards the hollow.

This had happened to Kes before and he knew what to expect, but for Lizzy the plunge into the gateway was terrifying. She knew she was screaming, but she couldn't hear her voice above the rush and roar as they all hurtled through the magical tunnel. The terror went on and on until she thought it would last forever. Then suddenly, in an explosion of water, the three of them surfaced in the rainbow cave.

'*Aaaahhhh . . .*' Lizzy's last cry of fear faded away into utter silence as she found herself bobbing in the water of the pool. Stunned, she stared around, trying to take in her first sight of the cave with its strange mirrors and shifting rainbows of light. But she was so shocked that nothing made any sense.

'Lizzy!' Kes swam to her. 'Lizzy, are you all right?'

She gulped, and struggled to get her breath back. 'Y-yes . . . I think so . . . What *happened*?'

'We've come through the gateway.'

Above them, a voice said, 'Indeed you have.'

Lizzy jumped as if she'd been stung. In the first

confusion of their arrival she had not noticed the rock couch at the pool's far edge. Now, though, she looked up and gasped.

Taran was reclining in her usual place on the couch, looking more regal than ever. Her seaweed cloak shimmered with tiny mother-of-pearl shells, and the golden circlet was on her head. She was every inch the Queen, and Lizzy was overawed.

Taran saw her expression and laughed. 'Welcome back, Kesson,' she said with mock sweetness. 'And this, I presume, is Tegenn?'

'She's called Lizzy now,' Kes said. Tullor hissed a warning, and hastily he added, 'Your Majesty.'

'Is she?' Taran smiled. 'How very *human*. But then she isn't really one of us any more.' Her green eyes glinted as she turned her gaze on Lizzy. 'Are you, my dear?'

Lizzy swallowed but didn't reply, and the Queen's smile faded a little.

'When I speak to you, Tegenn – or Lizzy, if you prefer – I expect to be answered. Mermaid, or human? Which are you?'

Angrily Kes thought, *She's playing a game, trying to frighten Lizzy just for fun.* But Lizzy had gathered her courage, and said in a voice that only quavered a little, 'I think I'm both, Your Majesty.'

'Both? Well, perhaps. But I see very little of the mermaid about you. Though . . .' She put her head on one side and studied Lizzy carefully. 'You do look a bit like your mother. Not as pretty. But then, compared to me, even Morvyr is plain and dull, don't you agree?'

Lizzy's heart was pounding. 'You are . . . very beautiful, Your Majesty.'

That pleased Taran and she laughed again. 'Your sister has better manners than you, Kesson! However, I did not summon you here to find out how polite you are. You have the silver pearl. I know, because only the silver pearl can open the gateway through which you have just come. Where is the pearl, Lizzy?'

Lizzy hesitated, then slowly raised her clenched hand. 'It's here . . . Your Majesty.'

'Show me!'

Slowly and reluctantly Lizzy opened her fingers
to reveal the pearl. Taran's green eyes lit hungrily
and she gave a great sigh, leaning forward and
staring as if she could hardly believe what she was
seeing. Tullor hissed, and at once the Queen's
gaze snapped to him.

'Leave us!' she commanded. 'I will call you
when I want you again.'

The eel dipped his head obediently. 'As Your
Majesty wills,' he said, and with a last spiteful
glare at Lizzy and Kes he slid under the water and
disappeared.

Taran looked at the pearl again. A smile spread
across her face and she laughed softly. 'Come
here, Lizzy. Give the pearl to me.'

Lizzy started to swim towards the rock – then
paused. Could they trust Taran to keep her
promise and set Morvyr free? She had to have
some reassurance.

She said, 'I want to see our mother first.'

Taran blinked. 'What?'

'I want to see our mother.' Kes pinched her

96

warningly but Lizzy took no notice. With Tullor gone she felt more confident, and she bravely held Taran's angry stare. 'It's only fair.'

'Fair?' said Taran. '*Fair?* It would be perfectly *fair* if I imprisoned your mother for the rest of her life for stealing the pearl from me in the first place!'

'She didn't – *ow*!' Kes had pinched her really hard this time, and Lizzy gave a yelp of pain.

Before she could recover, Kes said hurriedly, 'Please, Your Majesty, don't be angry with Lizzy! She didn't mean to be rude, and she's very, very sorry. *Aren't you, Lizzy?*' He gave her a third pinch and added humbly, 'It's just that she's worried about Mother. We both are.'

The trick worked. Taran hesitated, then her angry expression was replaced by a disdainful smile.

'Very well,' she said. 'I will overlook it this once. And because I am generous and merciful, you may see your mother before you give me the pearl. In fact, she's very close by, and I expect she's been watching and listening.' Turning round, she raised one hand and pointed at the indigo mirror. 'There she is.'

The water behind the mirror swirled and became translucent. There inside the mirror was Morvyr. When Kes had last seen her there she had been under a sleeping spell, drifting in the water and unaware of anything. Now, though, she was awake. Her face and hands were pressed against the mirror's surface and her grey eyes were wide as she stared out at Kes and Lizzy.

'Mother!' Lizzy cried. Morvyr's mouth was working but no sound came through, and in dismay Lizzy looked at Taran.

'You can't hear her,' said the Queen, 'though she can hear you. When I have the pearl, I will let her go. Now, give it to me!'

Morvyr started to shake her head wildly. She was calling out, and Lizzy saw her lips forming the word 'No!' over and over again.

'I'm sorry, Mother,' she called back. 'But you're more important to us than the pearl! I *must* give it to the Queen!'

She swam to the rock where Taran sat, and held out her hand. Again the silver pearl seemed to squirm, as if it, too, were protesting. Smiling broadly, Taran plucked it from her and held it up.

'Ahhh!' Her sigh of satisfaction echoed through the cave. 'After all these years . . . at last the silver pearl has been restored to its rightful owner!'

Chapter Nine

Behind the mirror, Morvyr burst into tears. Lizzy was nearly crying too. She felt like a complete traitor for going against her mother's wishes and giving the pearl to Taran. But there was simply no other choice.

Kes swam to the rock to join her, and put a comforting arm round her shoulders. 'It's all right,' he said. 'What else could you have done? Mother will understand.' He looked up at Taran, who was holding the pearl in one hand and stroking it with the other. 'Please, Your Majesty, will you set Mother free now?'

'What?' Taran had lost interest in the twins and

looked annoyed at Kes's interruption. Then her expression became more pleasant. 'Well, of course I will, Kesson. I promised, didn't I? A Queen *always* keeps her promises. Besides, what could I possibly want with her now?'

A sweet smile had appeared on her face as she spoke, and Lizzy felt a shiver go through her. She didn't trust this. *What could I possibly want with her now* . . . Lizzy knew the answer to that question. This sudden kindness was a sham, for there was only one reason why Taran was going to let them all go. She hoped that they would lead her to the black pearl.

Taran turned towards the indigo mirror again and made a careless gesture with one hand. The mirror's surface trembled, then in an instant it dissolved, sending an explosion of water cascading outwards with a noise like a huge wave crashing on a shore. Morvyr was flung out with it; twisting helplessly in the air, she bounced off the rock ledge before plunging into the pool in a flurry of flailing arms, tail and hair.

'Mother!' Gasping as the splash of her landing nearly overwhelmed him, Kes swam to her with Lizzy right behind him. Morvyr surfaced, and the twins flung their arms round her.

'Mother, oh, Mother!'

'Are you hurt?'

'I'm – I'm all right . . .' Morvyr righted herself and stared dazedly at them. Her eyes still brimmed with tears. 'Oh, children, what have you done?'

'We're sorry, Mother, but we had to!' said Kes pleadingly. 'The Queen said if we didn't give her the pearl, we'd never see you again!'

All three of them were trying to hug each other at once, but Taran's voice made them stop and turn.

'What a touching reunion!' the Queen drawled mockingly. 'But, Morvyr, you should be thanking your children, not scolding them. After all, they saved your life.'

Morvyr's eyes blazed but she tried to hide her anger. 'Then I *do* thank them for that, Your

Majesty. But not for the way they were made to do it!'

Taran laughed. 'Unlike you, they are sensible enough not to try to defy me. And now that I have the eighth pearl my power is greater than ever. You are no more use to me, so you may all go free. I will send you back through the silver gateway . . . but before I do I am *sure* you would like to see the pearl restored to its proper place.'

Her smile was triumphant as she removed the golden circlet from her head. Holding up the silver pearl, she touched it to one of the two empty settings, and began to whisper a chant that echoed softly through the cave:

'Seven you were; eight you are;
Nine you soon shall be,
As the royal crown is strengthened
By the power of moon and sea!'

The seven pearls in the circlet began to glow brightly, and Morvyr gave an anguished moan.

'Silence!' Taran snapped. Morvyr covered her face with her hands but said no more, and Taran's chant continued.

> 'I bind you once, I bind you twice,
> And three times with this sign.
> When the circle is completed,
> All power shall be mine!'

Light flashed from each of the seven pearls in turn, and the corresponding coloured mirrors flashed too. Red – orange – yellow – green – blue – indigo – violet – it was like being in the heart of a rainbow, and Lizzy and Kes gasped. Then as the wild glory of the colours dimmed, an eighth and far brighter flash dazzled through the cave. Its brilliance blinded them momentarily – and when their vision returned to normal, they saw that one of the two darkened mirrors had lit up and was shimmering like molten silver.

'*No . . .*' Morvyr whispered. '*Oh, no . . .*'

Taran held up the circlet. The silver pearl was

back in its place, nestling in the setting as though it had never been removed. All eight of the pearls were glowing softly, their colours reflecting in the eight shining mirrors. And only one mirror was dark and empty.

'It's done,' Taran said. She looked down at the three in the pool, and her face was cruel. 'You may go back to your homes and your lives. But never *ever* forget that I am your Queen. And when I have found the black pearl – as I surely will – *no one* will ever be able to challenge my rule!'

She touched the silver pearl and stroked it. Then she raised one hand and pointed to the centre of the pool.

The water began to swirl as a current sprang up from the depths. It caught hold of Lizzy, Kes and Morvyr, and they were dragged under the water, spinning and turning with the eddy. It pulled them down, faster, deeper – Lizzy thought she heard Taran's far-off laughter – then they plunged into the dark tunnel of the gateway. Lizzy's senses were thrown into mayhem. She had lost her hold on

Morvyr and Kes; she didn't know which way was up or down or right or left – all she knew was that she was tumbling over and over in a mad, whirling rush that she thought would never end. Then, so suddenly that she let out a yell of shock, she was flung out of the gateway and into the open sea.

For several seconds she kicked and flailed in confusion. But then a voice called her name, and Morvyr was there beside her, hugging her tightly and steadying her.

'Oh, Mother!' Lizzy clung to her, struggling to be calm. 'Kes – where's Kes?'

'I'm here.' Kes sounded shaky and his face looked dead-white in the underwater gloom. But he wasn't hurt. None of them were, which seemed like a miracle to Lizzy.

A shrill sound echoed through the water, and two dolphins came streaking towards them. Arhans and her companion whistled with relief as they arrived, nosing joyfully at Morvyr and the children. But then Morvyr's eyes widened as Arhans communicated a message.

'Jack?' she said. 'He's *here*?'

'Mother, there was no chance to tell you before!' said Kes. 'Father came with us, in a fishing boat – he's waiting for us on the surface!'

'Oh!' Morvyr's face lit like a star. 'We must go to him! I must see him! Show us, Arhans – show us where he is!'

Arhans whistled again and turned; Morvyr swam after her, and Kes and Lizzy followed. But Morvyr and the dolphins were setting such a pace that Lizzy couldn't keep up. Kes, looking over his shoulder, saw her struggling but failing to swim faster, and hung back to wait for her.

'It's all right,' he said. 'We'll catch up with them soon enough. Come on.'

Lizzy felt desperately disappointed. She so wanted to be there at the moment when Morvyr and Jack were reunited. If only she could unlock her lost self, and change into a real mermaid! But, though she tried with all her willpower, she still couldn't make it happen.

The light above them grew brighter as they

headed for the surface, then suddenly they burst out into sunlight and wind. Kes touched Lizzy's shoulder and pointed.

'Look,' he said softly.

The *Regard* was about thirty metres away. The small inflatable boat where Rose had sunbathed had been lowered over the side, and Jack was climbing down the hull ladder into it. Morvyr was swimming to meet him, and over the sound of the *Regard*'s gently pulsing engine the twins heard her calling his name.

Lizzy felt her throat constrict with emotion. She remembered how wonderful her own first meeting with Jack had been. But how much more wonderful it must be for Morvyr, after so many years of loneliness.

She looked at Kes, and knew that he understood and felt the same as she did. Then she felt his fingers link with hers and squeeze them.

'Come on,' he said, 'let's go a bit further away. I think they ought to have this moment to themselves, don't you?'

She smiled and nodded. Jack was in the inflatable boat now; he started the outboard engine and turned the little craft towards Morvyr. Lizzy and Kes let the current carry them away until they were a good distance from both the boats. As Jack reached Morvyr and held out his arms to her, Lizzy blinked rapidly and looked away from them to the *Regard*. There was no one on deck, and she couldn't see whether Mr Treleaven was still in the wheelhouse.

'I've got a feeling Mother will forget to be angry with us now,' Kes said quietly. He was grinning, though it was a weak grin, and Lizzy gave a little laugh.

'Let's give them a few more minutes on their own,' Kes added. 'And then we'll go and join them . . .'

Chapter Ten

In the cave of the rainbow pool, Taran gloated. She knew that Tullor was eager to come back, so that he too could see the silver pearl returned to its rightful place in her crown. But he could wait. She wanted to savour this moment of triumph alone.

She had taken the circlet off again and was turning it round and round in her hands. How wonderfully the pearls shone. How lovely their colours were, and the silver one added its own special radiance. *So* beautiful – and so powerful too. She could feel new power radiating from the circlet, and she revelled in the feeling. She was almost invincible now.

Almost . . . but not quite.

Suddenly a frown made Taran's face ugly. One pearl still eluded her. She was sure that Morvyr didn't have it; her cave had been searched thoroughly and it had never been found. But did she know where it was? By letting her and her silly children go free, Taran hoped to trick Morvyr into thinking that she was no longer of any interest. In which case, Morvyr might be foolish enough to lead Taran to the greatest prize of all – the black pearl.

The mermaid Queen stopped turning the circlet and stared at the silver pearl as something came to her mind. The silver and black pearls had special qualities. They could sing – Tullor had heard the silver pearl when Morvyr had shown it to the twins – but when either one sang, if the other were close by, it would answer!

Her green eyes widened and she held the circlet up to her own face as her fingers started to stroke the silver pearl.

'Sing!' she whispered eagerly to it. '*Sing!*'

*

'Oh, Jack, I can hardly believe it!' Morvyr was crying and laughing at once. 'First our daughter, and now you have come back! Our family is complete again!' Then her lovely eyes clouded. 'But Taran has the silver pearl. And if she finds the black one –'

'She won't,' Jack reassured her. 'She doesn't know that I'm here and, even if she did, she doesn't realize that I've got the black pearl.'

'Is it truly safe?' Morvyr asked.

'Yes.' Jack touched one hand to the locket round his own neck, the one he had made for Kes. 'It's here, where it's been since I went away.'

Morvyr reached out and touched the locket too. She was sitting close to Jack, balanced on the curved side of the inflatable boat with her arm round his shoulders. 'Could I . . . see it?' she asked. 'Just to be sure?'

He laughed gently. 'Of course, my love. I understand – seeing is believing, isn't it?'

He opened the locket, then stroked the inner surface. The secret compartment sprang open, and there inside, glowing darkly, was the black pearl.

Morvyr's face lit with wonder and relief. 'Oh, I'm so glad!' she said softly. Then she looked at Jack again and her voice became urgent. 'You see, there's another reason why Taran must never find it! When I was imprisoned –'

She stopped abruptly and they both stared in shock at the locket.

The black pearl had begun to sing. Its haunting note sounded clearly above the surge of the sea, and Morvyr's delight turned to horror.

'It's Taran!' she cried. 'Close the locket, Jack, *quickly*!'

Jack was already snapping the locket shut. The singing note stopped instantly, and he and Morvyr looked at each other in alarm.

'She must have told the silver pearl to sing!' Morvyr whispered. 'And the black pearl answered! If she's heard it – Oh, why didn't I *think*?'

'The locket was only open for a few moments,' said Jack. He was trying to reassure her, but his expression gave him away. 'Maybe there wasn't enough time for her to hear.'

'But, if she did, she'll know that the black pearl isn't far away, and she'll come looking for it! She'll stop at *nothing* to get hold of it! Jack – what are we going to *do*?'

In the undersea cave, Taran's green eyes seemed to catch fire as a second clear, piercing note rang out and echoed from the walls.

'*It isn't far away!*' Her voice was a grating hiss as she realized that the black pearl was answering the call of the silver. Suddenly the second note cut off – but it was enough.

'Tullor!' she screamed. '*Tullor!*'

The giant eel had been lurking just beneath the pool's surface, and as she called for him he rose from the water. 'Majesty! Majesty, what is wrong?'

'I told the silver pearl to sing, and the black pearl answered!' she screeched. 'It's here; it's nearby!' Panting, eyes wild, she got a grip on herself. 'We must find it, Tullor. We must find it, *now*!'

Grasping the circlet, she stroked the silver pearl, then pointed to the pool. Again the water started to swirl as the gateway opened. With a powerful flick of her tail Taran launched herself from the rock. 'Follow me!' she snarled. '*Quickly!*'

She and Tullor both dived, and moments later there was nothing to show where they had been.

'Jack, the children!' Morvyr cried. 'If Taran should come – Kes and I can escape, but Lizzy –'

'I'll look after her! Go now, Morvyr – go close to shore; Taran won't dare follow you there! I'll bring Lizzy back, and Kes can meet us at the harbour! *Hurry!*'

Pausing only to plant a hasty kiss on his cheek, Morvyr plunged into the sea and headed to where the twins waited. 'Kesson!' she called. 'To me!'

Two bewildered faces looked back at her across the grey-green swell. 'But, Mother –' Kes started to call back.

'There's no time to explain! Your father will look after Lizzy – come, *now*!'

Jack was already starting the dinghy's outboard engine. It coughed, spluttered, failed; he pulled the cord again, then a third time, and at last the engine came to life with a staccato roar. Kes was swimming to meet Morvyr. As he reached her, Arhans and the other dolphins appeared, surrounding them like guards, and they all streaked away, leaving Lizzy treading water alone in the sea.

'Lizzy!' Jack yelled. She couldn't hear him above the noise of the engine, but it was obvious that something was very wrong. The dinghy swung round and powered towards her, and she struck out for it. She was tired; swimming seemed to take a huge effort, but the boat was coming closer –

Suddenly the water behind Jack churned and foamed white. Lizzy saw it and cried a warning, pointing. And, as Jack turned his head to look, Tullor erupted from under the sea. His head rose three metres from the surface, his body writhing like a snake's. His cruel gaze scanned the water around him – and fastened on the dinghy.

A savage hiss ripped from Tullor's throat as he recognized Jack. He lunged towards the boat, and frantically Jack twisted the throttle lever fully open. The dinghy's nose went up and it bounced madly across the heaving water.

'Lizzy! Lizzy, get in!' Jack closed on Lizzy but had to slow down as he reached her. He swung the boat in a wide half-circle, one hand stretching out. Lizzy made a desperate grab; their hands locked and he heaved her bodily out of the water and over the dinghy's rubber side.

'Crouch down and hang on tightly!' Jack shouted, twisting the throttle again. Lizzy flung herself forward and clamped her fingers round the mooring line as the boat raced over the sea's surface. They were heading for the *Regard*, but Tullor was behind them and closing. Daring to glance up, Lizzy saw his shape rearing like a dark shadow and she stifled a scream of terror. Then suddenly a larger shadow fell across the dinghy – she heard the deep throbbing of the *Regard*'s engine and was almost thrown out of the dinghy as it bucked in the trawler's wake. They sped round *Regard*'s stern to the starboard side, and Jack powered the dinghy towards a rope ladder that dangled down from the rail.

'Go, Lizzy!' The dinghy bumped against the *Regard* as he throttled back to match the trawler's speed. Lizzy didn't need telling twice. She grabbed the short ladder, and with a shove from Jack to get her started she went up like an acrobat and fell sprawling on the trawler's deck. As she raised her head, winded, she came face to face with Paul.

Paul had finished his task, then gone to the galley to make another brew of tea. He was coming up to the deck with brimming mugs in his hands when Tullor appeared. Paul's jaw dropped at the sight of the monstrous eel – and what was Lizzy doing flat out on the deck, soaked through and in her wetsuit?

Paul and Lizzy stared at each other. Paul's mouth was working but he couldn't speak, and Lizzy didn't know what to do or say. Then Jack came to the rescue.

'Paul!' he bawled. 'Grab the painter and lash the dinghy on! *Quick!*'

Paul was enough of a seaman to react automatically, and as the dinghy's mooring line came snaking through the air towards him he slammed the mugs down and grabbed it. Jack cut the outboard engine and came up the ladder after Lizzy. Paul was still gaping, but before he could splutter out any questions, Mr Treleaven shouted from the wheelhouse, 'Get the trawl out! We'll show that snarlywig what's what!'

Jack headed for the trawl gear, while Paul hastily secured the dinghy's rope and hurried to help him. Lizzy started to scrabble to her feet – then her eyes widened as they focused on the sea.

'Jack, *look!*'

Tullor still reared above the water, though he was keeping well clear of the trawler. And someone else had come to the surface beside him.

'It's Taran!' Lizzy yelled. Jack, though, had already seen the mermaid Queen – and Taran had seen him.

'*You!*' Her furious cry carried across the water, and she turned on Tullor. '*He's* got the black pearl! Attack him – *attack him*!'

Tullor hissed with fear. Fishing boats were one of the few things he was afraid of, and he didn't want to obey. Taran's face contorted with rage and her voice rose to a shriek. '*Do as I order you! ATTACK HIM!*'

Tullor hesitated, but he was more frightened of his Queen than he was of the *Regard*, and he launched himself after the trawler in a whirl of spray. The slow beat of the trawler's engine suddenly speeded up, the boat surged forward and as the giant eel ploughed towards it Jack shouted, 'Now, Paul!'

There was a rattling din from behind Lizzy, and she jerked her head round in time to see the trawl net go snaking over the stern. The churning wake swept the net away from the *Regard* as Tullor caught up – and Lizzy heard his frenzied snarl as he plunged straight into the mesh. It closed around him; he thrashed wildly but his struggles only entangled him more thoroughly.

'We've got him!' Jack's shout of triumph carried to the wheelhouse. Paul was still goggle-eyed as he stared at the writhing eel, but he kept his wits enough to help pay out more of the net.

'Good work!' Mr Treleaven called, grinning. 'Now stop the trawl, and let's see what else we can catch!'

With Tullor writhing helplessly in tow, the *Regard* began to turn, and Taran saw that it was heading straight for her. Her mouth opened, but suddenly she realized that the trawler would be on her before she could use magic against it. If she weren't to be caught like Tullor, there was only one choice she could make. She flung a glare of pure hatred towards the oncoming boat, and vanished under the sea.

The *Regard* sailed relentlessly on over the spot where Taran had been, but the mermaid Queen was gone. Behind the boat Tullor still struggled in the net, and Lizzy slowly climbed to her feet. She was shaking all over and still could hardly breathe. Everything had happened so *fast*; she could hardly take it in, could hardly –

The thought collapsed as she turned round and came face to face with Rose.

Rose was at the top of the steps that led down to the cabin. Her face was white – but not from sea-sickness. She stood frozen, mouth agape and eyes wide, and she was staring at Lizzy as though she were a total stranger.

'Rose . . .' But there was nothing Lizzy could say. She didn't know how much her sister had seen. But the shock on Rose's face gave the answer away.

She had seen everything.

Chapter Eleven

For a few moments that seemed to last forever, Lizzy and Rose stared at each other in numb silence. Lizzy thought: *I can't face it. I can't even try to explain, not now!*

'Lizzy . . .' Rose began in a tight, tiny voice.

Lizzy whirled round and stumbled away towards the stern. She heard Rose call after her but she took no notice, and clung to the rail, watching Tullor thrashing in the water. The trawler had slowed down, and Jack and Paul were at the winch.

'What on earth is it?' Paul yelled over the noise of the winch motor. 'What's going on?'

'There's no time to explain now!' Jack shouted back. 'Just make sure he can't escape!'

They hauled in one end of the net so that it closed like a bag round Tullor. The giant eel was now trussed and powerless, and Paul stared at their prisoner in amazement. 'I've never seen anything like it!' he said. 'And I thought I saw –'

He was interrupted by Mr Treleaven, who had hurried from the wheelhouse. 'I've put the helm on automatic,' he said. 'Let's have a look at him, then . . .' He peered over the stern and whistled. 'He's *enormous!*'

'Yes, and he's far too big and dangerous to haul on board,' said Jack breathlessly. 'We'll have to tow him back to port.'

'Right!' Mr Treleaven agreed. 'Keep him well astern – we don't want to risk fouling our propeller!' He looked at Lizzy, and his expression was full of understanding. 'Don't worry, love,' he added. 'This brute won't be troubling you again. I know just the place for him. Paul!' Paul looked up, and Mr Treleaven continued, 'Get on your mobile as soon as you can, and call the Sealife Centre. Tell 'em we've got the biggest snarlywig for them that they've ever seen!'

'Right . . .' Paul blinked and nodded, and Lizzy echoed, 'Snarlywig?'

'It's what we call conger eels around here. Suits him, doesn't it?' He patted her shoulder. 'You'd better go below, change that wetsuit for some dry clothes and have a hot drink. We'll be home before you know it!'

Lizzy started to turn, and stopped as she saw that Rose was still standing motionless on the cabin stairway.

Jack had seen too. 'Ah . . .' he said. 'She saw what happened, then?'

'Yes . . .' Lizzy looked helplessly up at him. 'What am I going to do?'

Jack sighed. 'You'd better tell her the truth, Lizzy.' He hesitated, then smiled encouragingly. 'You said you wanted to. And I think she'll believe you now, won't she?'

Lizzy's heart was bumping under her ribs. But

Jack was right. She had longed to share her secret with Rose. And she had promised that, as soon as she could, she would tell her sister everything.

She swallowed something that was trying to stick in her throat, and walked slowly along the deck to where Rose waited.

'Lizzy . . .' Rose's eyes were wide with wonder and confusion. 'That eel . . . and − and there were other people; they looked like . . . like . . . *mermaids*!'

'Yes,' said Lizzy quietly. 'They were.'

Suddenly Rose's paralysis snapped and she grabbed Lizzy's arms, almost shaking her. 'I wasn't dreaming, was I? I *saw* them! And you were in the sea; you were with them! *Lizzy, tell me what's going on!*'

Lizzy took a deep breath. 'All right,' she said. 'But you might want to sit down . . .'

Rose leaned on the rail and stared out over the sea as the *Regard* chugged steadily homeward. She hadn't said a word for several minutes, and

Lizzy watched her uneasily, waiting for her to break the silence between them.

At last, Rose did. 'I shouldn't believe a word of what you've told me,' she said in a quiet voice. 'It's totally nuts, totally insane, and I shouldn't believe it. But I saw Kes and . . . and Morvyr. And I saw the other one; the one you said is the Queen. And you were swimming in the sea with them, just as if you lived in the water, and the dolphins were there too, and . . .' She blinked, and shook her head vigorously as if to clear it. 'I've *got* to believe, haven't I?'

'I didn't at first,' Lizzy told her. 'I felt just the same as you. But when Kes showed me that I could breathe underwater . . .'

'That must have been incredible.' Rose managed a wan smile. 'And it kind of . . . proves that magic is real, doesn't it? It's weird, but even at my age I sort of . . . hoped it was . . .'

There were tears in her eyes, and Lizzy knew why. Rose was thinking of her own real parents, who had died when she was too young to remember them.

'I'm not jealous,' Rose went on suddenly. 'Honest, I'm not. You've found your real mum and dad, and that's *amazing*. I just wish . . .' She stopped again.

'I wish it could happen for you as well,' Lizzy told her gently. 'Oh, Rose – if only it could come true for you the way it has for me!' Suddenly, impulsively, she gave Rose a hug, putting all her strength into it.

'Yeah, well.' Embarrassed, Rose wriggled free and wiped her eyes with an impatient hand. Her fingers clenched and unclenched on the rail, and when she spoke again her voice was almost back to normal.

'I'd really like to meet her. The mermaid. Your –'

'Morvyr.' Lizzy smiled. 'I'd like that too, and I'm sure she would. I'll ask her.'

Rose nodded. 'Will she be OK? I mean, if the Queen's that evil, she might try to do something to her and Kes.'

'Jack says the dolphins will look after them,' Lizzy told her. 'And they're going to stay closer to shore. Taran won't come anywhere near the land in case humans see her.'

'I'd probably feel the same, if I were in her shoes.' Then Rose gave a funny little laugh. 'That's a crazy idea, isn't it – a mermaid with shoes!'

Lizzy smiled. 'And we've got Tullor,' she added. 'He's the meanest of all Taran's servants, so with him out of the way there isn't so much danger.'

Rose glanced towards the stern where the great eel was being towed behind the boat. 'What are they going to do with him?' she asked.

'I heard Mr Treleaven telling Paul to ring the Sealife Centre. I think they'll take him there and keep him in a tank.'

'I suppose that makes sense. Provided they've got a tank big enough!' Then Rose seemed to rally her thoughts, and her uncertain expression changed to a smile as she suddenly became her usual brisk, breezy and slightly bossy self again. 'Come on,' she said. 'Here we are in the middle of just about the coolest adventure anyone could

imagine, and we're standing here being all serious.
Go and get changed, then let's go to the front of
the boat to see which one of us spots land first!'

There was a reception committee waiting on the
quay when the *Regard* nosed into her berth at the
harbour. Two people had driven over from the
Sealife Centre on the north coast in response to
Paul's phone call, and Paul had texted just about
everyone he could think of to spread the news of
the astonishing catch. The local coastguards and
several of the lifeboat crew were there too,
together with a small crowd of holidaymakers
who had seen all the activity and come to find out
what was going on.

Tullor had given up trying to free himself and
now lay quiet in the net, his cold eyes glaring
furious hatred at everyone who came to stare at
him. When he saw Lizzy he opened his mouth in
a menacing snarl that showed his razor teeth.
Lizzy looked quickly away.

The Sealife Centre people – a young woman

and an older man – came aboard the trawler to
see how best they could get Tullor out of the sea.

'We've phoned for the water-tank truck, and it's
on its way,' the young woman said. 'I just hope
it'll be big enough! I've *never* seen a conger eel
this size – he's an absolute freak!'

'He'll be our prize exhibit,' the man added.
'Once the news gets around, people will be
coming from all over the country to see him.'

'It'll be safe, won't it?' Lizzy asked anxiously. 'I
mean, if he broke out or anything . . .'

'Don't worry,' said the woman cheerfully. 'Our
tanks are strong enough to stand up to anything
he can do.' She put her fists on her hips and
stared around the deck. 'Right, then. We'd better
start thinking how we're going to winch him up
and get him in the truck!'

Lizzy moved out of the way of the bustle of
activity. Jack was by the wheelhouse, and he came
over to her.

'We can leave them to it. Kes is here – over by
the lifeboat station.'

'What?' Lizzy spun round and looked across the harbour. There in the distance a small familiar figure was standing on the low wall that ran alongside the station building.

'They're safely back!' Her face lit with relief. 'Oh, thank goodness!'

'Shall we slip away and join him?' Jack suggested.

'Yes!' Then Lizzy saw Rose watching them from a few metres away. 'Could we . . . I mean, do you think Rose could come too?' she asked hesitantly.

Jack smiled. 'I'm sure that'll be all right. After all, she's one of the family, isn't she? Come on; let's take her with us.'

Rose was very quiet as the three of them left the *Regard* and walked towards the lifeboat station. As they approached, Lizzy saw dismay in Kes's expression, and she ran to him ahead of the others.

'It's all right, Kes – Rose knows about us!'

'She *knows*?' He looked horrified.

'I had to tell her. She saw what happened.

Mother, and Taran – she saw everything. But I know we can trust her.' She hesitated, then added, 'She's always been my sister, remember.'

'Yes . . .' Then a look of wonder flitted across his face. 'I suppose, then, she's sort of my sister too, isn't she?'

'Of course she is!' Lizzy grabbed Kes's hand as Jack and Rose reached them, and turned with a huge smile. Jack was beaming as well; he hugged Kes so hard that he was lifted off his feet, then said, 'Is your mother safe too?'

Kes nodded. 'She's gone to one of the quiet little coves beyond the beach. Arhans is with her.' He nodded towards the quay. 'What's all the fuss down there?'

Jack grinned. 'We've got Tullor.'

'*What*? You *caught* him?'

'We certainly did.' Jack told the story in a few sentences, and Kes heaved a thankful sigh. 'That's brilliant! Taran won't be half so dangerous without him to do her dirty work for her!' Then his expression changed. 'Father, can you go to

Mother now? She wants to see you as soon as she can.'

'Of course! I'll borrow Jeff Treleaven's sailing-boat; he won't mind.'

'Can I come with you?' Lizzy asked eagerly. Then she paused and glanced at her sister. 'And Rose . . . she so much wants to meet Mother. Do you think –'

'No!' Kes interrupted quickly. The others all stared at him and Jack began, 'Kes, she knows the truth about us all now. And Lizzy says we can trust her.'

Kes reddened. 'It isn't that. I'm sorry, Rose. I didn't mean . . . but we ought to ask Mother first. You see, Father, there's something else – something she found out when Taran was holding her prisoner.'

Jack frowned. 'I remember – when we were out at sea she started to tell me there was another reason why Taran mustn't get hold of the black pearl. But she didn't have time to explain.'

'She wouldn't tell me about it,' said Kes. 'She

says she has to talk to you. It's really important –
and it's got to be kept secret.'

'It's OK,' Rose said. 'I understand. If you want
to tell me later, fine. But I'm not going to be
nosy.'

She shrugged carelessly as she spoke, but Lizzy
knew she was unhappy. It was hardly surprising.
So many exciting things were going on, and Rose
wasn't really part of it. She felt left out and hurt,
and Lizzy was sorry for her.

Jack did too, but Kes's news had to come first.
'Look, Rose,' he said, 'I think we'd better go and
see Morvyr on our own, Kes and Lizzy and me.
Do you mind very much?'

'Course not,' said Rose lightly. 'And don't
worry; I won't say anything to anyone else, either.'

'Thanks, Rose.' Jack smiled warmly at her, then
turned to the twins. 'Come on, you two – we'd
better get going. Kes, if you come in the boat with
us, you can show us where the cove is.'

'Cool,' said Kes, then grinned. 'I learned that
word from Lizzy!'

He and Jack set off towards the marina where Mr Treleaven's sailing-boat, *Silvie*, was moored. Lizzy hung back, though, and when they were out of earshot she turned to Rose.

'We *will* tell you everything if we can,' she promised, then added: 'After all, like Kes said, you're my sister, so you're sort of his too.'

Rose looked startled. 'Did he say that?' Her face relaxed and a weak smile appeared. 'I hadn't looked at it in that way before, but I suppose it's true . . .' Then she punched Lizzy's arm affectionately. 'Go on, hurry up and follow them, or they'll leave you behind!'

Lizzy flashed her a grateful look that said more than words, and ran after Kes and Jack.

Chapter Twelve

With her mainsail hoisted, *Silvie* sped with the wind across the bay and headed up the coast towards the cove where Morvyr was waiting. Kes was fascinated. He had never been in a boat before, and he wanted to know the proper names for everything on board. He was thrilled when he was allowed to take over the tiller for a while, and asked eagerly if Jack would teach him to sail.

'Of course I will,' said Jack happily. 'Lizzy's learning about living under the sea, so it's about time you started learning about life on land!'

Lizzy looked at Jack. 'You're not going to go away again, are you?' she asked.

He smiled reassuringly. 'No. I'm home. And I mean to stay.'

They reached the cove in a little over half an hour. It was a tiny, sandy inlet, almost hidden between the folds of the cliffs. As they approached, Lizzy saw what looked like the wake of a speedboat heading towards them, then Arhans appeared beside the boat, whistling a greeting.

'Arhans!' Lizzy leaned over to stroke the dolphin. Then, a few metres behind her, Morvyr surfaced.

'Jack! Oh, Jack!' Morvyr raced to the boat, and Jack reached to help her in. She was breathless, and though she hugged him joyfully, it was obvious that she was very worried.

'Kes says you've got some important news,' Jack started to say, but Kes interrupted.

'Mother, Father and Lizzy have got news too! They've caught Tullor! They brought him back to harbour, and he's going to be put in a tank and kept there!'

'Oh!' Morvyr's eyes lit. 'That's wonderful! Without him to threaten us – but, Jack, what I've discovered is even more important.' She paused, drawing a deep breath. 'Kara's daughter, Karwynna, is alive!'

There was a stunned silence as all three of them stared at her. Then Jack said urgently, 'Are you *sure*?'

'I'm certain! When I was trapped behind the mirror I heard Taran talking about her to Tullor.' Quickly she repeated everything Taran had said, finishing, 'That's why I was so upset when the children gave Taran the silver pearl in exchange for me! It's more important than ever now that she doesn't have all the pearls, because, if she does, she'll kill Karwynna!' She turned to Lizzy and Kes. 'Karwynna's safety is much more important than mine – oh, children, if only I could have warned you!'

'It wouldn't have made any difference,' said Kes fiercely. 'We'd still have given Taran the pearl if it was the only way to free you, wouldn't we, Lizzy?'

'Yes!' Lizzy agreed. 'Getting you back was the only thing that mattered!'

'But –'

'Morvyr, don't be angry with them,' said Jack. 'You're much more important to them than Karwynna is.' He smiled. 'And I feel exactly the same as they do.' Then his face became grave. 'But it's vital that the black pearl is kept safe from Taran now. She knows I've come back, and she must realize that I've brought the pearl with me.' He paused, thinking. 'She said she would fetch Karwynna from her prison? But where is that prison? Where is Taran keeping her?'

'There are so many possible places,' said Morvyr unhappily.

'I know. We need some kind of clue before we can even start searching.'

'But we *will* search, won't we?' Morvyr asked passionately. 'If we can find her and rescue her, all the merfolk will join us and we'll have a real chance to defeat Taran once and for all!'

Jack nodded. 'Yes, we'll search. But we mustn't

tell anyone else what we've discovered yet, or
Taran might find out that we know about
Karwynna. It's going to make the task harder, I
know, but we have to do this on our own.' He
gazed around. 'This cove should be a safe place
for you and Kes to stay. The entrance is narrow,
so the dolphins can easily guard it.' Arhans
whistled agreement, and Jack added, 'Taran might
try to kidnap you again, to make me give up the
black pearl. So you must be *very* careful from
now on.'

Again Arhans whistled, and slapped her tail
down hard on the sea's surface, splashing them
all. Kes smiled at Lizzy, who was looking uneasy.
'Don't worry. Arhans says that she and her friends
will guard us night and day. We'll be all right.'

'And Taran hasn't got Tullor to help her now,'
Jack reminded them. 'That'll make it more
difficult for her. She'll be plotting and planning,
but I don't think she'll do anything yet.'

'So we just have to wait for her to make a
move?' Kes asked.

'Yes. She will, we can be sure of it. But it'll take time. And we can use that time to look for clues that could help us find Karwynna.'

Morvyr's eyes met his. 'Do you think we *can* find her?'

He took hold of her hands and squeezed them. 'I believe it. And if you believe it too, and believe hard enough, then we *will*!'

Silvie, with Lizzy and Jack aboard, left soon afterwards. Two of the dolphins escorted them, and Kes and Morvyr waved from the cove until the boat was out of sight.

Lizzy was very quiet as they sailed back towards the bay. Her mind was filled with tumbling thoughts. Where was Karwynna? Could they find her? What would Taran do next? She wanted to ask a hundred questions, but she knew that Jack had no answers. As he had said, they would just have to wait.

They passed the little lighthouse and headed towards the harbour. Jack adjusted the sail to set a course for the marina and, as they approached, Lizzy saw someone standing by the pontoons.

'It's Rose,' she said. 'She must have waited for us.' Uneasily she looked at Jack. 'What am I going to say to her?'

Jack thought for a moment, then smiled. 'I think you can tell her everything.'

'Really?' Lizzy's eyes lit eagerly.

'Yes. If you say we can trust her, that's good enough for me. She's your sister, after all.'

Lizzy gave him an adoring look. 'Thank you! I *so* much want to tell her. She's been really brilliant, and I did promise that I'd explain as soon as I could.'

'Then you go ahead. Just make sure that *she* promises not to say a word to anyone else at all. Not even Paul.'

'She won't. Not if I ask her to promise. She'll help us too, if she can.'

'I'm sure she will. Look, she's seen us.'

Rose had started to walk along the pontoon. Lizzy waved, and Rose lifted one hand, uncertainly, in reply. *Silvie* nosed into her berth, and Rose reached them as Jack was tying up to the mooring ring. 'Hi,' she said hesitantly. 'Is everything . . . OK?'

'Everything's fine.' Jack smiled a reassurance and helped Lizzy on to shore. 'And Lizzy's got a lot to tell you.' He winked at Lizzy. 'Go on, off you go, you two. I'll just make sure the boat's secure, then I'm going back to the Treleavens' for a well-deserved rest!'

The girls said goodbye and walked away. As they reached the lifeboat station, Rose said, 'I've been thinking a lot while I waited for you. Everything that happened today . . . It's all so weird, I can still hardly believe it.' She glanced at Lizzy. 'But it *is* true, isn't it? I didn't dream it?'

'No, you didn't dream it.' Lizzy laughed self-consciously. 'I felt the same as you when I first found out. It's real, though. All of it. And like Jack said, there's loads more to tell you.'

Rose looked back to where Jack was furling *Silvie*'s sail. 'He's really nice,' she said wistfully.

'I know.' Lizzy hesitated, then decided to be

brave. 'He's my real dad, and that's wonderful. But it isn't going to make any difference to you and me, Rose. After all, we've both got another dad, haven't we? And a mum too. They're my parents, just as much as Jack and Morvyr. We're all a family.'

Rose stared at the ground for a moment, then looked up. There was a tell-tale glitter in her eyes, and her make-up had started to smudge. 'Yeah,' she said, then abruptly her face broke into a grin. 'And now, little sister, you're going to tell me the rest! Come on, I want to know *everything* that's happened!' She linked Lizzy's arm firmly in hers. 'Seriously, are things OK now? Is it all over?'

'All over?' Suddenly Lizzy wanted to burst out laughing. She knew it was just a reaction, and she squashed it with an effort and returned Rose's smile instead. 'No way,' she said. 'In fact . . . things are probably only just beginning!'

Epilogue

Tullor lay in a crevice of artificial rock, glaring with hate-filled eyes at the faces peering into the tank in the Sealife Centre. Every day, for hour after hour, crowds of humans gathered to gawp at him, goggling and pointing and chattering – he hated them! He wanted to lunge at them, bite them, tear them to pieces with his savage teeth! But the tank's glass wall was too strong, and when he had tried to batter through it he'd only hurt himself. So he hid as best he could in his cranny, while the hatred seethed in his mind.

The long day ended at last. The last of the humans shuffled away, the lights were turned off and he was left in peace. There were no other creatures in the tank with him, for he would have quickly caught and eaten anything smaller than himself. But Tullor didn't care about that. He had been waiting for the quiet and darkness. For he had work to do.

He concentrated his thoughts, drawing on his fury to give him extra power.

Majesty . . . It is Tullor . . . It is Tullor . . . He sent out the silent call from his mind, and listened for an echo in the silence. Could the Queen hear him? Would she answer? Perhaps she was angry with him for failing her. But she had ordered him to attack the fishing boat, and that was why he had been caught in the trawl net. Surely she would answer him, if she could!

Majesty . . . I need your help, Majesty . . . I am your faithful servant; if you will help me, I can still be useful to you! It is Tullor, Majesty . . . Tullor . . . Tullor . . .

Then, very faintly, he felt something stirring in the depths of his mind. It seemed to come from far, far away, but it was a sound, a whispering, like a distant, dreamlike voice.

Tullor's long body tensed, and his eyes lit fervently. Then he opened his mouth and hissed with triumph.

I am your servant, Majesty! Command me, and I will obey!

The whispering was clearer now, and he strained to hear and understand. The sound in his head went on for a long time before at last it faded. When it had finally gone, Tullor lay in the darkness, staring at the world outside. It was beyond his reach, but that didn't matter now. Because *she* had heard him, and *she* had work for him to do. He must just be patient for a little while longer.